Here's what people are saying about *The Beauty of Being*

"Abiodun Oyewole is a born storyteller, a real griot. I've been waiting for this book for a long time. When you read his stories in *The Beauty of Being,* most of them personal and touching, it's like you can hear him telling them to you in his warm and melodious voice. This book is not only a historically relevant book, especially when he writes about The Last Poets and Malcolm X, it is also a book full of wisdom."

—Christine Otten is a Dutch writer, journalist, performer, and the author of *The Last Poets* (2016)

"*The Beauty of Being* is a spiritual journey. From the jungles of Central America to the jungle of New York City's Harlem, these tales are of one man's journey through life, with his beloveds meeting angels and nature on its own terms, plunging back and forth from the abyss to paradise."

—Baba Donn Babatunde, percussionist of The Last Poets

"As a former member of the Harlem Committee for Self-Defense, we sponsored Malcolm X's birthday celebration in Mount Morris Park, so we "birthed" the Last Poets and witnessed their growth close up. Founding member Abiodun Oyewole was a natural storyteller, but he was different than the other poets. While all of them gave us enlightenment, his infectious smile and laugh gave us immense JOY in living our blackness. His ENLIGHTENED JOY is truly contagious and fully present in *The Beauty of Being,"*

—Gaye Todd Adegbalola, blues musician

The Beauty of Being

The Beauty of Being

A Collection of Fables, Short Stories & Essays

ABIODUN OYEWOLE

Introduction by Felipe Luciano

NEW YORK

www.2leafpress.org

P.O. Box 4378
Grand Central Station
New York, New York 10163-4378
editor@2leafpress.org
www.2leafpress.org

2LEAF PRESS
is an imprint of the
Intercultural Alliance of Artists & Scholars, Inc. (IAAS),
a NY-based nonprofit 501(c)(3) organization that promotes
multicultural literature and literacy.
www.theiaas.org

Cover art: Annelie Solis
https://www.anneliesolis.com/

Book layout and design: Gabrielle David

Library of Congress Control Number: 2017963109

ISBN-13: 978-1-940939-74-2 (Paperback)
ISBN-13: 978-1-940939-83-4 (eBook)

10   9   8   7   6   5   4   3   2   1

Published in the United States of America

First Edition | First Printing

2LEAF PRESS trade distribution is handled by University of Chicago Press
/ Chicago Distribution Center (www.press.uchicago.edu) 773.702.7010. Titles
are also available for corporate, premium, and special sales. Please direct inqui-
ries to the UCP Sales Department, 773.702.7248.

To Ace, with love.

CONTENTS

Ode to Abiodun

"The true sign of intelligence is not knowledge but imagination."

—Albert Einstein

LIKE AN ORCHID THAT SLOWLY opens up its delicate petals to the sun, I've witnessed over these past fifty years the transformation of Abiodun Oyewole: the poet, the teacher, the father, the friend, and the intellectual.

The metamorphosis of his being and spirit was not cataclysmic; it was subtle, slow, and quiet. There were no political announcements, no debut party heralding his ascent into the sacred space of "elder." He just kept writing and teaching and holding Sunday school poetry sessions in his Harlem apartment with the new ones, those political babies The Last Poets helped bring into this world. And what a father he has been, with his own children as well as with his "adopted" kids: calm, non-judgmental (unless the shit gets stupid), reassuring, and inspirational.

The Beauty of Being, A Collection of Fables, Short Stories and Essays, is a peek into Abiodun's maturation.

How he learned to "si" life away from the bustle of Harlem. How true love softly rained on his budding petals through an extraordinary woman named Judy "Ace" Stafford. How the Sun of Truth, the earth of the ancestors, and the air of imagination gently pushed him into the vulnerability of manhood, and the ability to see himself and the world in Latinos, in Africans, in anybody. And yes, they didn't have to be black.

If you could travel in a time capsule back to 1967, you wouldn't think this was possible. Not this man. Not this fiery Black Nationalist whose poems of righteous indignation shouted in a *basso profundo* voice drove audiences crazy, almost delirious. I've seen men cry, women throw themselves onto auditorium floors writhing in ecstasy or guilt or something. Abiodun has the ability to shake you to your core, spiritually, politically, and physically.

The Beauty of Being reflects just that, the simple joy of living in the moment. It takes courage to leave his comfortable Harlem nest and travel around the world without even knowing the language, but Abiodun does it all the time, and he never seems to tire of it. His writing reflects the joy of discovery with the guarantee that no matter what happens, you're going to learn something, something that will enhance your "being," making you wiser, compassionate, and more loving.

What's more, these stories are like pieces of fabric from the tapestry of Abiodun's life. They are quiet and simple, like the country people he writes about in this body of work. Whether he is in Senegal, Costa Rica, Mexico, the Ivory Coast or Harlem, Abiodun tells stories in a Hemingwayesque rhythm without trying to make a point; you figure it out 'cause he already worked it out in his head, and has already applied it as a life lesson.

This Meistersinger, who has all the requirements for a doctorate, doesn't care about validation. Instead, Abiodun Oyewole cares about people. He cares about every young black person he mentors, every Latino he encounters, every friend he touches, who in turn feels his wisdom, his love and his intelligence. What more validation does one need?

To have endured the pounding gauntlet of being a black man in America, to have survived and to have succeeded is Abiodun's message to black people and to the world. All of us need to take that journey inside to grow and discover "the beauty of being." ■

—Felipe Luciano
New York, NY
April, 2018

Beauty is not in the face;
beauty is a light in the heart.

—Kalil Gibran

CHAPTER 1

The Tree Of Life

YEARS BEFORE CURIOUS was born, his grandmother had planted a tree in the backyard. Even as a little child, Curious loved to sit under the tree and listen to the birds sing. The most outstanding feature on the tree, however, was the golden flowers that stayed in bloom all year round. Curious' mother had told him that her mother didn't want anyone to pick not one flower from the tree. "If you pick just one flower, it will die" she said.

Growing up, Curious remembered what his mother said. He never picked a flower from the tree, but he would touch the velvet softness of its petals. He would feel the softness against his cheek and entertain his nose with its sweet fragrance. Quite a few times, Curious thought about plucking a flower just to see what would happen to the tree. He thought to himself "If I pick a flower and the tree dies, it would be a real tragedy because the tree has been in the family for years. And people come from many miles to admire the tree and take pictures, to see this big sturdy tree with wide green leaves and golden flowers on its branches, even in the middle of winter."

Some people called it a miracle tree. It was thought throughout the neighborhood that the tree also brought good luck. Everyone in the vicinity of the tree was prosperous. The people attributed this wealth to the tree and keeping Grandmother's wishes in reverence. Then along came Passion. She had moved from another town with her family. Her father had heard about the tree, and after seeing it decided it would be wise to move into the neighborhood.

You see, Passion's father was a wealthy businessman who was always on the hunt to capitalize on everything. "Making money is the only thing that matters in this world," he would often say. And you'd think Passion would have been a fat girl because she just couldn't get enough of anything, On the contrary, she wasn't. She had a beautiful brown, well-shaped body, and a tantalizing smile. Curious was stunned the moment he laid eyes on her. He had never seen anyone like Passion, and had the kind of good feelings he never had before. They became instant friends.

"There's only one thing as beautiful as you, Passion," Curious told her, "and it's the tree."

"You think I'm only as beautiful as a tree?" she sniped.

"No I didn't mean it like that," he exclaimed in an apologetic way. "You're more beautiful than any tree anywhere in the world.

"Prove it." Passion replied.

"Prove it but how?" Curious asked. He suddenly grabbed her, and pulled her close to him. She didn't resist. He brushed his lips against her face, her neck, her naked shoulders. She looked seriously into his eyes. His mouth found the cleavage of her breast. She stopped him.

"If you really think I'm more beautiful than the tree pick me a flower." Passion said.

For a moment he thought anything he gave her would never be enough, but he was willing to try to somehow please her. Out of his drunken lust for her, Curious came to his senses. "You know if anyone picks a flower from the tree, the tree dies," he told her. "I could not put that shame on myself."

"You say I'm more beautiful, yet you won't pick a flower from the tree for me because of something your grandmother said?"

"It's more than something she said," he replied. "The tree would die."

"I can't believe that you Curious, of all people, wouldn't want to know whether it was true that by picking one little flower that the tree would die." Passion added, "Even if it dies, it will live again. Nothing dies forever. Everything always comes back to life."

Curious listened to everything Passion said. Yes, he had thought about picking a flower from the tree long before Passion came along, but this was different. He could prove his love for Passion if he just picked a flower from the tree.

It was a little after dark when Passion went home. The sun had gone down, and only the tree with the golden leaves glistened in the evening shade. Curious sat underneath the tree. He decided he'd have a talk with his grandmother and ask her what to do.

You see, Curious thought he had already figured it out. He knew the tree and his grandmother were one in the same, and taking a flower from her branches would be like taking a finger from his grandmother's hand. Curious could not see himself doing that. But then suppose Passion was right. Suppose it's true that nothing dies forever and everything is reborn in some form or another. He thought long and hard and eventually fell asleep underneath the tree.

In his dreams, Curious spoke to his grandmother, and explained to her that if you really love someone, you want to do something special for them. How could it be wrong if it's done in truth. We're all human and should adorn ourselves with everything nature has provided.

So he decided.

When Curious woke up, he walked around the tree trying to decide which flower he should take. He didn't want it to be so obvious. It's just one flower for Passion, not a whole bouquet. Then he saw the perfect flower nestled in between two wide leaves. No one will notice it's gone, he thought to himself, unless, of course, the tree dies.

Later that evening, he couldn't sleep, he was too excited. He couldn't wait to see Passion, and give her the golden flower that he had carefully placed in a little box. In the morning, Curious ran to Passion's house. She was sitting on the porch when he arrived. It was as if she knew he was coming.

"I have something for you," he said smiling.

"You did it Curious!" Passion exclaimed. "You did it for me. Oh let me see."

He handed her the box and she peeked inside. She took the flower out and placed it in her hair. Curious was amazed at how the flower seemed to enhance Passion's beauty even more.

"This is the first time I ever got something I really wanted, "Passion said, elated. "Thank you, Curious." She leaned forward and kissed him gently on the lips, a kiss he would never forget.

When the folks in the neighborhood saw Passion's flower, they came to see if the tree was dead.

"The old lady didn't know what she was talking about. The tree still lives," they all said. Passion's flower created envy, and every young woman had to have a flower.

Soon, everyone came to pick flowers from the tree, Even Passion's father picked quite a few with the thought of selling these exotic flowers for a lot of money. By sunset, every single flower on the tree had been picked. All that was left were the sturdy branches, and those wide leaves that somehow looked abandoned.

When Curious and Passion looked at the tree, he now understood what his grandmother was trying to do. She knew as soon as one person picked a flower, others would do the same. So for generations, no one had until now. Passion and Curious stood there in each other's arm's looking at the now naked tree where beautiful golden flowers once stayed in bloom all year around. The tree looked sad.

"You think it will ever grow flowers again?" Curious asked Passion. "You said nothing dies forever."

Passion was saddened by the moment. She felt maybe she had done something terribly wrong, asking Curious to pick a flower. Now her flower was no longer special. Just about every young woman in town had one. She ran to the tree and hugged it.

"Please grow flowers again." Passion pleaded "I'm so sorry this happened but I know you can live again." ∎

CHAPTER 2

A Night in the Jungles of Costa Rica

COSTA RICA IS A LOVELY COUNTRY in Central America. It's sandwiched in-between Nicaragua and Panama, and has all the lushness and sunshine of any island in the Caribbean. The people are Mexican looking and very friendly.

What's special about Costa Rica is that they don't have an army (although they do have a small military force in all but name only), so the government concentrates on their infrastructure, like education and communications. You can feel the peace in the air. The beaches are nice, and the casinos are generous. Judy and I had become casino players. Judy played the slot machines, and I played Black Jack. We both did pretty well in Costa Rica.

Since Judy was an avid reader, she knew all the places of interest we should check out—she was the best co-pilot anyone could ever have. So this latest adventure entailed driving to the other side of the island to find the river where the turtles are born. It was that time of year for the baby turtles to appear on the shores of the river, and for some reason, we thought this was something worth seeing.

We drove through this heavily dense forest for about an hour looking for this river. Then we came to a little wooden bridge that didn't look like it was meant for cars or anything too heavy to drive on. It looked so precarious; I stopped and got out of the car to check out the bridge a little more closely. It was suspended by thick ropes, which really made us both think about turning around and going back. I looked over the side of the bridge, and it looked like a hundred foot drop onto rocks and water. We sat there awhile wondering if we should take a chance or not. Then all of a sudden a mini-bus appeared full of children laughing and talking. It never hesitated, and went right across the bridge. We took a sigh of relief and decided to drive across, thinking we were heading in the direction of the river.

We rode down dirt roads, through banana plantations, and a forest so dense it looked like a jungle. It had obviously been raining earlier because there were a lot of puddles along the way. There were no houses in sight, nothing but forest. We finally came across some people, and asked them if they knew where the river was. They didn't know. Or maybe they didn't know what we were talking about. Even though I speak and understand a little Spanish, communicating was a problem.

I saw a banana farmer and asked him. I said *adelante*, which I thought meant straight ahead, and he nodded his head like that was the way to go. So we got back in the car and went in that direction across more puddles. Then we came to this real big puddle that covered the entire road. Since this still looked like a path, I thought maybe we could ride through it, but I was wrong. The puddle became a swamp, and the car started going down. We were shocked. Judy's bag was in the swamp and hundred dollar bills were floating. I shouted to Judy, "Go swim and get the money!"

The front end of the car had quickly become sub-merged in the swamp. We knew this was trouble with no-body around to help us in the middle of nowhere. After we retrieved our things, we got out of the car and started walking—with absolutely no idea of where we were going. I then thought it would probably be best to head back to that store, since that was the only sign of life we saw. Then we saw a man with a backpack. He spoke no English, but motioned for us to follow him, and we did. It was late after-noon, but there was still enough light for us to see.

With all that was going on, I started getting hungry. The man stopped, and looked through his backpack—I just *knew* he had some fruit or crackers or something to munch on that he was going to share with us. I waited with great anticipation as he pulled a flashlight out of his bag. *A flash-light!*

Besides being thoroughly disappointed that there was no food, I quickly realized that the flashlight signaled that we would soon be walking in the dark, a prospect I was not looking forward to, but what else could we do?

By the time the sky had darkened, we came across what looked like a rebel camp. He took us inside one of the wooden shacks. There were guns leaning against the wall, and young men sleeping with mosquito nets around them. One of the young men took us to a vacant shack, and pointed to a big trough of rainwater as if to say that was the water we would have to use. On the way to our little shack, I saw warning signs about mosquitoes with a skull and bones symbol, and told Judy these mosquitoes are se-rious out here.

Our little shack had nothing but a couple of wooden planks together that we used as a bed. I covered myself and Judy as best I could with our beach towels, so we wouldn't get bitten. We had weed on us, but we didn't even think about smoking it, because we didn't know what would happen next.

We were in survival mode.

We tried to go to sleep, but we could hear the rain beating against the roof. At least we had shelter from the rain even though it sounded menacing as it pounded the tin roof. With all of this going on, I couldn't help but think about the car in all this rain. It might be completely submerged in water tomorrow.

Somehow we fell asleep.

Early the next morning, we were awaken by a sound at the door. It sounded like a gorilla. We got real quiet, and then the sound went away. We both were afraid to see what it was, but we had to get up and get out so we could rescue the car and get back to civilization. We had destroyed our sandals walking over rocks, branches and rough terrain in the swamp, but it was a miracle we didn't break or sprain an ankle.

I opened the door cautiously and went outside.

I looked around, but I didn't see anyone so I started searching the ground for some kind of footwear, and found some old sneakers. I actually found two pairs. One pair fit me perfectly, but the other pair was small. I cut the toe out with a sharp object, and gave them to Judy. At least the bottoms of her feet would be protected from the rocks.

I figured we should walk back to the car, and then maybe walk back to that general store we had stopped at the other day to get help to pull the car out of the swamp. As we walked through the campsite, we didn't see any of the men from the night before. It looked like the whole area had been turned into a lake; there was water everywhere. In the daylight, we had a better sense of where we were, and it seems we were in a banana plantation—banana plants were everywhere.

We finally arrived at the car.

The car was still there, tipped into the water front first with the motor and front seats submerged in water. After surveying this mess, Judy and I decided to go back to the store we had passed the other day to get some help. We had both gone to summer camp when we were kids and did some hiking as part of camp activity, but nothing nearly as rigorous as this.

We both sighed in relief when we finally arrived at the store. When the woman inside saw us all muddy and wet she quickly told us in Spanish and sign language to take off our clothes so she could wash them. She gave us something to wear in the meantime. After we changed I decided to go next door, which I discovered was a work area because I could see some men working with the bananas.

I asked if someone had a truck that could pull our car out of the swamp. No one spoke English so communicating our situation was a bit difficult. At first I wasn't getting very far, but then a young man appeared who could speak English. I explained to him what our problem was, and told him we needed a vehicle to pull the car out.

He understood.

He told me he had a pickup truck and offered his help. Our angel's name was Tony, and he recruited two other young men who seemed eager to help. Tony got some thick rope, and told us to jump in the truck so we could go get the car.

After a couple of false starts and delays we were finally on a mission, and I was beyond grateful. And for the first time, I was beginning to feel confident that we could actually save this car. Judy remained behind with the women who were busy preparing food; they even had her shucking peas. Before I left, I told her she looked like one of the natives, and we both chuckled, because no matter where we went, we could always rely on the kindness of people.

We arrived at the car. It looked so pitiful face down in the swamp. Tony and the young men got to work immediately. I sat on the car's rooftop watching them while they tied the rope around the back bumper. While I was sitting there, I could clearly see that this really was a jungle. There were all kinds of animal life, like snakes and lizards swimming in the water, and a little black gorilla with a yellow stripe down his back was sitting in a tree, watching me. It was scary to think that Judy and I had not once, but twice, walked through this swamp, and managed not to be attacked by the creatures who lived in this environment. The ancestors were with us for sure, I thought.

They started pulling the car out. At first it wouldn't budge. Tony revved up the motor and tried again, but this time the big thick rope popped. I couldn't believe it.

This was not going to be easy.

The men looked at the bumper, spoke for a moment in Spanish, then one of them ran off, but soon returned with a chain. They wrapped the chain around the back bumper, and on the first try pulled the car out of the swamp. It was a mess as it was covered with mud all over the front, but the back of the car hadn't been affected.

Tony asked. "Do you have the keys?"

I was too afraid to find out if it could start so I threw the car keys to him.

Tony got in the car and turned the key. I could not believe it. It started up right away. I was so happy.

When we arrived back at the store, I was riding in the passenger side and Tony was driving. I gave Judy a thumbs up when we rolled in. The children there could see the car needed cleaning so they, along with a teenager who could drive, took the car somewhere where they could wash the mud off. Everyone was so helpful.

While the car was being cleaned, I sat down with Judy to shuck peas and socialized with the people. We were treated like family. Judy took Polaroid shots of everyone there. They were all fascinated by the pictures coming out so fast. She also gave them a new can opener that they appreciated very much. When the car returned it was clean like it had never been in the swamp. We were totally impressed with the work the children had done, so I gave each child some money, and they were very happy.

By this time, our clothes had dried in the hot sun, so we changed and prepared to leave. After we said our goodbyes and got in the car, we realized that the seats were soaked. We pulled out the beach towels, and sat on them. Since we had the car for another week, I was hoping that somehow we could dry out the front seats.

We decided to drive to Puntarenas on the Pacific side of the island where the sun seemed to be a bit hotter. After we opened the doors in hopes of drying out the seats, I decided to look under the hood, and was surprised to see the motor all covered with mud. At first, I thought about cleaning it off, but then I realized they (the rental service) never look under the hood. They only look in the trunk where the spare tire is. I was actually scared to wipe the mud off the engine, because I had this eerie feeling that if I wiped the mud from the engine, it would cease to function. We had enough adventures for the past couple of day. *I left the mud on the engine.*

While we spent a rather uneventful afternoon trying to dry the seats out, I started thinking how lucky Judy and I were. We spent the night in the jungle, but we didn't get hurt or bitten by mosquitoes. The car was stuck in the swamp, but we found people who were wiling to help, and now we're riding in it. I felt someone was watching over us, which drew me to what I felt was a logical conclusion: since we had been so lucky maybe it was time to see if this luck would hold up in the casino.

We drove back to San Jose and went directly to the casino. I was right, Lady Luck was still with me. In no time, I had won eight hundred dollars, and was feeling pretty invincible. I gave Judy eight black chips to hold for me, and told her she would be the bank until I cashed them in. Each black chip was a hundred dollars each.

I was on a winning streak, and couldn't lose, *but I should have known better.*

I should have known better because everything comes in cycles. I had my luck and it was time for me to go, but instead I stayed. I had convinced myself that my good luck would never run out, and if it did it would only be temporary and come back quickly.

I started losing like I had been winning.

As they say "You got to know when to hold them, and you got to know when to fold them."

I thought I could overrule all of that and allowed my arrogance get in the way. The money was disappearing as fast as I had won it, so I asked Judy for some of the chips I had given her. She said they were stashed away. I persisted, but she refused. Then I pushed it up a notch, and began demanding. When I angrily said, "Don't let me make a scene in this casino," Judy gave me all of the chips and stormed out of the casino. And I, having finally gotten my way, proceeded to lose everything I had won.

I felt so stupid, but I had only myself to blame.

I truly got carried away, and didn't think about the fickleness of Lady Luck. When we left the casino, I so was pissed off. I drove the car down the highway in a rage.

Judy asked "What are trying to do kill us?"

"Yes" I said.

When we arrived at our hotel, I was still heated. I knew I had some money in the room, since there was a casino in the hotel, I was determined to get my money back. I parked the car and slammed the door and left Judy behind, forgetting that she had the key to our room. So I went to the front desk, but instead of getting another key I used my credit card to get five hundred in cash. Then I went straight to the casino.

There was only one table open, and an older white lady was playing. When I sat down to play I knew she wasn't too thrilled about it, but I really didn't really care. I was on a mission to get some of my money back. After two or three hands, the lady left. So it was just me and the dealer.

I did pretty well. I won about half of what I lost at the other casino, so at least there was some sign of redemption.

We had a couple of more days in Costa Rica before it was time to return home. I still couldn't help but think about what we had gone through with the car being stuck in the swamp, and us stuck in the jungle. We had survived a wild experience. Now the real test was when went to return the car.

When we got to the rental car place, the attendant checked the car all over. I prayed he would not open the hood. He never did, but he did ask why the seats were so wet. I told him I left the windows open all night while it was raining. He looked at me strangely, but there were no extra charges.

I was so taken by the fact that that car could still be driven after such an ordeal, I decided I would try to sell the story to Nissan. I spoke to the advertisement department at Nissan and even told the lady the story. After I finished she agreed it was a fantastic story, but then she said "We have our own writers. Thank you. I felt silly because I had just given them a story for their writers for free. A few months later I saw pieces of the story played out in a commercial. ∎

CHAPTER 3

From Acapulco to Ixtapa and Back

ACAPULCO IS AN INTERESTING CITY that was initially designed for tourists. Acapulco was once one of Mexico's top beach resorts, but age and scattered violence has dimmed the city's glitter just a bit. One of the bright spots is La Quebrada, where you see these brown Mexicans jumping off a hundred foot cliff doing a perfect dive into the water. The divers must calculate the right moment to jump to catch an incoming wave. It's really a sight to see because there are rocks below, and if they do not land in the water, it could be a horrible tragedy.

Judy and I were there as we watched one diver after another doing what looked like a swan dive into the water. A pretty big crowd had gathered to see the event. Everyone was amazed.

Mexico is also known for elaborate churches. One could easily surmise that these people are devoutly religious. Judy and I would always visit at least one house of worship during our travels and say a prayer, and Mexico was no exception. In fact, some of the best artwork I've seen in my travels happens to be in a house of worship. Catholic Mexico has no end of exquisite churches, cathedrals, temples and ex-convents for intrigued travelers like Judy and I to take a look at; some feature unique and eclectic architecture, while others have outstandingly ornate interiors.

Judy and I rented a car. It was really a Jeep with no doors, which made it rather risky—one bad move and you could fall out of a moving vehicle. Seatbelts weren't mandatory back then, and I don't believe they had seatbelts in any of their Jeeps. After we visited some churches and cathedrals, we decided we wanted to see more of Mexico, so we made plans to drive from Acapulco to Ixtapa.

Ixtapa was the wealthy section of Mexico. Ixtapa was nothing more than a coconut plantation until the late 1970s when the Mexican government's tourism development group decided that the Pacific coast needed a Cancún-like resort. In came the developers and up went the high-rises. The result is a long string of huge hotels backing a lovely beach, with a small community of well-to-do Mexicans living in the surrounding area.

Judy and I always enjoyed checking out where the rich folks live so we got ready for our adventure. We had our goodies: some rum and Coke, some herb, our beach towels, our music and each other, and soon we were on our way. We drove through Mexico's countryside. The roads were very well taken care of, and the scenery was mainly of trees and bushes alongside the road.

While we were driving, I noticed a soldier with a serious rifle in his arms. There was a pretty young girl standing on the side of the road near him. He motioned for us to stop. After I stopped, he and the young girl came over to the car to ask for money. It appeared she was in some kind of beauty pageant, and needed money to participate. My Spanish isn't great but I know *dinero* means money in

Spanish. Besides, the girl held a thin cylinder for people to deposit the money in. I quickly realized this was some kind of weird scam, and drove off.

After a while, I decided to stop to take a leak. I found a nice big bush, but about twenty yards away I heard voices so I walked to where the voices were. It was a mother bathing her daughter in the stream. I felt bad because I had invaded their privacy. I said excuse me, and started to leave when the mother said it was okay. They really did not seem bothered by my presence; the little girl was smiling and so was her mother.

Speaking in Spanish, the mother asked me where I was from. I told her I was from the U.S. She also asked for my name. I told her. She introduced herself and her daughter, then offered me some food, which was one piece of fish on a makeshift piece of tin on top a fire. I felt I would be taking more than they had to offer, and besides I wasn't hungry. I graciously refused, and explained I had to get back to my lady who was in the car waiting for me. They smiled. I smiled and waved goodbye. They waved back. I thought to myself, people all over the world can be so nice if you just let them be.

Judy and I finally made it to Ixtapa. It felt timeless and was a great escape of rolling mountains, and sparkling beaches. They had the most elaborate hotels, and the neighborhoods were very clean with lovely houses. We realized we weren't going to drive back to Acapulco that night, so we needed a place to sleep. We checked out a couple of hotels, but they were way too expensive.

At one point, we decided to sleep on the beach. Since the weather was great and the beach was empty, we thought this was a great idea, considering it wouldn't cost us a thing. We took our beach towels and other personal belongings and went to the beach, but found being on the beach in the dark was as scary as it was mysterious. I couldn't get comfortable and neither could Judy so, we immediately abandoned the idea.

We decided to walk around a bit, and ran across a big cow just walking down the street. I said "Moo," to the cow and to my surprise I heard a "Moo" back.

I knew it wasn't the cow, so I looked around to see who it was and saw two young men a short distance away with big smiles on their faces. They introduced themselves to us as Carlos and Benito.

"When we heard you 'Moo,' I said 'Moo' too just to keep the conversation going," Benito said. We all laughed. Then we told them where we were from, and what we were doing there. Benito and Carlos had driven down from Canada in a bus. We told them we were looking for a place to spend the night and they offered their bus as shelter.

We walked to their bus. It was dark, but we could see some Winnebagos, buses and vans. When we got to the bus, it looked like an ordinary school bus on the outside, but inside there was a cozy living room, a kitchen and a sleeping area. They had gutted the bus out and created a plush mobile home.

"This is amazing" I exclaimed.

"Now if you go out and come back in, make sure you step on the little rubber mat before you touch the door handle. Our security system is electrical."

The place was really laid out. Judy and I were given a bed in the area that was for sleeping. Benito showed us around, and even offered us food that was in the refrigerator. We had lucked out. For no money we had a cozy place to lay down our heads. We got a good night's sleep, and looked forward to a nice swim in the morning. When we awoke in the morning, we realized this was a trailer park with a lot of amenities. They even had a decent breakfast for just $1.50. We took a swim, had breakfast, and started preparing for our trip back to Acapulco. Benito said he wanted to go to Acapulco to see his father, and asked if it would be alright if he came back with us. Carlos was going to take the bus back to Canada. Of course, we welcomed Benito. After all, we had just spent the night in his bus. Besides, Benito seemed like a fun person, so I knew the ride back would be interesting.

We started our journey back with Benito and a bottle of wine. I also had some good Mexican weed to go along with the wine. We shared stories, laughed and just enjoyed each other's company. Every town we drove through, Benito would get another bottle of wine. He explained to us the young ladies on the roadside with the soldiers were candidates for a beauty contest, and they were intimidating motorist to give them money to help the girls enter the contest. That was a first for me and Judy.

We didn't have a radio or a cassette tape machine in the car so I sang a lot. Benito seemed to enjoy it as much as Judy did. I sang some original songs, and a lot of Carlos Jobim's songs. I guess we were having so much fun that I didn't realize I was getting drunk off of all the wine we were drinking. Driving was never an issue. *Drinking and driving is something I seem to do well.*

We finally arrived back in Acapulco. We went straight to Benito's father's house. He had a nice little place with a backyard. There was a hammock tied up between two trees in the backyard, so I decided I would get in it. I guess the alcohol was getting to me because I fell out of the hammock. When everyone realized I wasn't hurt, they laughed. I laughed too. *Drinking and driving has its limits.*

Benito's father was a short stocky man who had a keen sense of humor like his son. He didn't speak English, but we communicated very well.

"Que linda" he said when he saw Judy.

Being raised around Puerto Ricans in the Bronx comes in handy when you're in a Spanish speaking country. Judy and I knew he had just said Judy was pretty.

We ate some chicken, rice and beans for lunch, then I got back in the hammock and took a nice nap. Before Judy and I left, we exchanged numbers, and said we'd stay in touch.

We never did hear from Benito, and we never tried calling. That was a beautiful moment in time where human beings looked out for each other to create a blessed memory. ■

CHAPTER 4

The Tale of The Last Poets

It was Harlem New York in 1968
At a birthday celebration
For a man who was great
He was shot dead in the Audubon
Three years before
No one had a clue of what was in store
His words were very plain
And not complex
This man's name was Malcolm X
So in 1968 in mount Morris Park
Three brothers graced the stage
With Malcolm in their hearts
To be poetic disciples of his actions and deeds
These brothers recited poems
That gave power to black seeds
Power to recognize
We're the change we desire
Power to tell the truth
And set the world on fire
You see martin was killed April 4th of that year
And many black people were living in fear

It became very clear there was only one solution
It was to unify and have a revolution
A revolution that would give us power
To control our lives
A revolution that would inspire
All oppressed people to rise
Rise and respect the love and beauty that's within
Use these as our weapons
And through it all we will win
So on this day May 19th in 1968
Three poets made a pledge
That they could never escape
They pledged to each other
To be poetic voices for the revolution
They called themselves The Last Poets
This was the final conclusion
It started out with three poets
And one conga drummer
They had spears for tongues
They could turn winter into summer
They did poems about love and revolution
All in the same breath
Their words could help you be stronger
Or bring sudden death
They had a place in Harlem
They called it the East Wind
They knew the west was not the best
And the east is where life began
Just like the sun rises every day
The east wind gave birth that would never decay
Over time the poets changed
But the philosophy remained the same
They wrote poems to rearrange

This world that's gone insane
They wrote poems about niggers
And how we need to be black
They used their pen as a trigger
Because blacks were under attack
They said this is madness
And it must be stopped
We've suffered too much sadness
Like the blues is all we got
The Last Poets were loved
And appreciated everywhere
They set the stage for hip hop
Because they were brazen bold and bare
Now almost fifty years later
We come to tell this tale
Of a special group of black men
Who knew they couldn't fail
Using the word as a weapon
To change this situation
All together it was seven brothers
With a lot of dedication
They always had a heartbeat
Who was the conga player
To keep Africa alive
And become the demon slayer
The names of these men
Should not be left out
It was their courage and will
That made it all come about
David Nelson was the one
With the idea
He gave the group its name
And said turn a tear into a spear

Gylan Kain gave the group a black aesthetic
How to write sassy black poetry
And poetically describe the tragic
Felipe Luciano a Puerto Rican in the crew
Recognizing his African connection
To make his life so true
Umar bin Hassan
Who brought the funk to the mix
Talkin bout niggers are scared of revolution
That's too much for them to fix
Jalal Mansur Nuriddin
Was the master of rhyme
He'd weave some words and sounds together
That could really blow your mind
Sulaiman El Hadi
Was a true storyteller
Using rhyming verse
To teach you things you need to know and do
Abiodun Oyewole a poet with passion for his people
Willing to do what's necessary
To make the playing field equal
Nilija the first heartbeat
From the beginning he was there
To speak the language of the drum
So the message you would hear
Babatunde is the present heartbeat
That keeps the group alive
He like Nilija are Shango priest
That provides that African drive
Together they are all last poets
To announce our place on earth
Using words in rhythm poetically
This is what The Last Poets gave birth

CHAPTER 5

The St. Thomas Episode

MY LADY AND I were vacationing on the luscious island of St. Thomas. This had become a tradition for
my birthday to be somewhere where there was sun, sand
and sea. Judy was my travel agent. There were times when
my money was short, so she would cover the charges.

Back in the day, there was an expression for best
friends, "ace boon coon." Judy and I adopted that expression and called each other "Ace." I loved vacationing with
my Ace.

So here we were on the Virgin Island of St. Thomas:
blue skies, turquoise blue water, soft white sand, and the
smiling sun. The people were brown and beaming in the
sun. The children were walking home from school, they
looked so orderly in their school uniforms. The beautiful
palm trees, coconut trees, and trees with flowers against
the background of pastel colored homes was breathtaking.
Every place looked like a post card. We rented a car and
started our adventure.

In the heart of town was a sign across the street announc-
ing the Moko Jumbie Festival that was coming up. A moko
jumbie is a stilts walker or dancer. Moko jumbie has been

a cultural symbol in the Virgin Islands for over 200 years, and is a tradition that can be traced back to Africa. "Moko" means healer in Central Africa and "jumbi" is a West Indian term for a ghost or spirit that may have been derived from the Kongo language word "zumbi." These stilt dancers are an integral part of island life, and can be found in entertainment venues, parades, troupes, and various other festivities.

The sign reminded me of a guy I met, Ali Paul who was a stilt walker in the festival. He also happened to be an important political official of the island. It seemed like everyone was gearing up for it.

We continued driving around the island taking in all the sights. There was a white kid with his thumb out asking for a ride. We both saw him and we both ignored him. We don't pick up white hitchhikers, and we weren't looking to start now. We drove down a street parallel to the sea.

Then we saw this house. It was special. It looked almost like it was suspended in space. It was built on a precipice overlooking the sea. There was a gate that clearly stated the property was off limits, but our curiosity got the best of us, and we had to investigate. So we parked the car, and climbed the gate onto the property.

It was really laid out nicely, surrounded by beautiful shrubberies and flower bushes. Everything looked well taken care of. But seeing the house from the outside wasn't enough. We had to venture inside, even though we knew we were breaking the law.

"Wow!" What a spectacular house.

We were standing in this big spacious living room with a huge glass wall over-looking the Caribbean Sea.

The view was breathtaking. The house looked like something out of Ann Rand's *The Fountainhead, a* house designed by Howard Roark. This was a house of the future with modern furniture and lovely decor.

Then all of a sudden out of nowhere, this big dog with snarling teeth showed up and behind it was a white lady with a butcher's knife. We immediately started telling the lady we were just curious and didn't mean any harm. Both of us were pleading our asses so we wouldn't get mauled or stabbed.

The ancestors must have been with us because the lady calmed down and let us leave without a problem. We got out as fast as we could, knowing that we had really just dodged a bullet, or should I say, a stabbing. The irony of it all was that as we were leaving the estate, the gate opened. It was the white hitchhiker we had passed earlier. He obviously lived there. If we had known, this could have been a completely different story.

We were very happy to be back in the car. "That was too close" Judy said "You're right about that."

Thank you ancestors.

We rode along silently, counting our blessings. ■

CHAPTER 6

The Birth of The Last Poets

ON APRIL 4, 1968, Dr. Martin Luther King Jr. was assassinated while standing on the balcony of the Lorraine Motel in Memphis Tennessee. He was there to help establish a union for the black sanitation workers. I felt a serious surge of anger. King was doing everything he could to help black people get equal rights in this country. Everyone knew his platform of non-violence.

I wanted to do something to avenge the killing of Dr. King.

David Nelson, a friend of mine, had spoken to me earlier about creating a collective of poets to address many of the issues that black folks were facing. Now with King's death, I was really anxious to get the collective started.

So on Malcolm X's birthday commemoration on May 19, David, Gylan Kain and myself, were in a program to read poetry in Mt. Morris Park at what would become a well attended gathering.

I was raised in Jamaica, New York in the borough of Queens, and I felt very insecure about reading poetry in Harlem. I had visions of the "Sandman" pulling me off the stage. Harlem was the center of black culture, not only in New York City, but the world. This was my first time reading poetry in front of a Harlem crowd, and didn't know if I could measure up.

It was a very large crowd, and I was hoping what I said would work.

I came to Harlem a week earlier just to get a feel of the people, and what I might write about. Plus, this was my first attempt at writing revolutionary poetry.

There was an expression going around at the time, "What is your thing?" "Thing" had become like a revolutionary pronoun to mean, "What is your participation in the movement?" "Are you a Black Panther or a Nation of Islam Muslim or affiliated with any other Black Power group?"

There was also a hit record at the time entitled, "It's Your Thing" by the Isley Brothers, so I decided to write a poem called, "What's Your Thing Brother." While preparing for the gig, I quickly discovered that black people are very poetic. Sometimes in passing you may hear a poetic statement just naturally flow out of the mouths of black folks because that's who we are.

On that eventful day, I met David at his apartment, which was right across the street from the park where we were going to perform. He told me we were to be joined by another brother he had heard at a Columbia University poetry reading named Gylan Kain. He was a dark brown-skinned brother of average height with an intense vibe. I figured since we were going on stage together, we should do something that would present us as a unit.

I offered a song, but Kain couldn't hold a note if you gave it to him. David could sing, but his voice was rather weak, so I decided we should chant together. I had heard this chant by Howard University students, who were demonstrating against their president. The chant was "Are you ready niggers, you got to be ready." We agreed that we would walk on stage together chanting this. By the time we reached center stage, the entire crowd was chanting with us, which immediately established us as a group that didn't even have a name. Kain's first poem was, "Niggers are Untogether People," David's poem was, "Are you Ready Black People," and mine was, "What's Your Thing Brother." Our first performance on that memorable day truly got us off and running.

Now that we had established ourselves as a poetic ensemble, we needed a name.

In fact, we got our first paying gig that same day to appear at New York University, but we *still* didn't have a name. David began doing research on a possible name. He read poems like, "Strong Men" by Sterling Brown, "For My People" by Margaret Walker, and several poems by Gwendolyn Brooks. But the poem that would give us our name was "Towards a Walk in The Sun," written by the South African poet, Keropatse Kgositsile. The poem talks about the horrid conditions blacks were living under apartheid. The last stanza encapsulated our mission:

> The wind you hear is the birth of memory
> when the moment hatches in time's womb
> there will be no art talk. The only poem
> you will hear will be the spear point pivoted
> in the punctured marrow of the villain; the
> timeless native son dancing like crazy to
> the retrieved rhythms of desire
> fading
> in-
> to
> memory."

David added as the last line:

> "therefore we are The Last Poets of the world."

We all agreed from that day forward to be known as The Last Poets.

HARLEM WAS A WONDERFUL PLACE to be a poet. There was so much going on all the time. Poems were popping up in my head every day. Since poetry is all about rhythm and imagery, I found myself in the center of a poetic experience just by being in Harlem. I guess Langston Hughes, who was from Joplin, Missouri, felt the same way when he made Harlem his home.

Kain was searching for a place for us to work out of. He found a loft space on 125th Street between Fifth and Madison Avenue. It was an L shaped loft he named "East Wind." Kain had been living in the Village, but now he was ready to relocate to Harlem.

I was the youngest in the group, but I was learning every day. David was connected with this new clothing enterprise named New Breed Clothing Ltd. One of the co-owners is credited with coining the term, "dashiki," and in keeping with the Black Power movement's efforts at black uplift and cooperative economics, they were very supportive of us and even gave us a place to rehearse. I also recall a brother named Clayton Riley, who spent a few hours filming us at a rehearsal.

I was really enjoying this black experience, of being in Harlem, and being a part of something significant. I would sometimes eat at Sylvia's, the most popular soul food restaurant in Harlem, and would explore other places and spaces throughout Harlem. One of the main attractions was the Apollo Theater, where great black talent got their start on Amateur Night, which still exists today.

To me Harlem was black and beautiful, a lot different than growing up in Queens. In Queens, people lived in private homes for the most part, and tried to stay private. In Harlem people were on the streets socializing, styling, and just being black.

One of the things I noticed almost immediately is that in Harlem, there was a liquor store and a funeral parlor on almost every other block. There were also some big beautiful churches in Harlem like Salem United Methodist Church, Abyssinian Baptist Church, and Southern Baptist Church, the church my parents brought me to every Sunday. I still had an apartment on Hillside Avenue, but I drove to Harlem every day in my beige 1966 Impala.

So now we had a name, The Last Poets, and a place, our loft the East Wind. *We were ready for the revolution.*

We gelled almost immediately. Being a poet during those times carried a lot of weight. It was like being a prophet or a soothsayer.

During this time, part of my personal growth was to experience new things and new ideas. *I was learning.* New Breed featured dashikis, and other African print apparel. Unlike mainstream fashion shows, where the models were white and skinny, and just walked down the runway, New Breed's fashion shows were *hot*. The models had bodies, shapely bodies, and they would dance and strut across the stage to the latest Top 40 hits of the day. I remember they had designed a suit for brothers where there was a pleated split in the back. They called it the "peacock flare" to accommodate a brother's backside. We were wearing Afros, cornrows, and dashikis. We were writing poetry, plays, and publishing our stories. We embraced African drumming and incorporated it into our dance and music. We were flipping the switch, promoting racial pride on our own terms. We were feeling good about ourselves, creating our own culture, and at the same time, becoming politically and socially aware, and empowering each other. *And a lot of this was happening at the East Wind.*

There was always something going on at the East Wind. We had political workshops, theater workshops and creative writing workshops. We even practiced martial arts there. The East Wind was becoming very well known, and The Last Poets reputation was getting bigger. We'd often performed at block parties, churches, and other black establishments.

We were busy. The revolution was heating up.

The Last Poets was not complete until we figured out what kind of music we should incorporate into our performance. We tried a number of musicians, a guitar player and a few conga players before we decided on Nilaja Obabi. Nilaja was perfect. He didn't just play the congas, he talked to us through his drums. He was a little below average height brown-skinned brother with enough energy to light up a town.

Nilaja became the heartbeat of The Last Poets. He would listen to the poem while you recited it, and then figured out a rhythm for your piece. No poem had the same rhythm. He enhanced what we did on stage tremendously.

We had the fever.

We were constantly creating new material. As our popularity grew, people would ask us to perform their favorite poems, like "Niggers are Untogether People," "The Possibility of Lovers," "Say Blackness," 'What's Your Thing Brother," "God Died," and "Run Nigger." Me? I was having the time of my life, but everything didn't always go so smoothly.

Kain and David were a few years older than me, and while I learned a lot from both of them, Kain tried to be my father, an idea I totally rejected. I had a father that raised me very well. I didn't always appreciate my father's disciplinary actions, but he did make a responsible man out of me, and for that I am forever grateful. Kain could never fill his shoes, and I wasn't looking for someone to fill them. *I wasn't looking for a father figure.* This often led to conflicts because I could become rebellious when someone challenged my "space." In doing so, the lines between guidance and plain out bossiness became blurred.

For example, once I wrote and typed up this two page poem called "Get Hip." It was all about putting the black middle class down. I read the poem to the group to get approval and add it to our repertoire, but Kain said, "We're not doing no crap like that in the group." I was crushed. I thought it was a very good poem. Plus, I had even taken the time to type it up.

I challenged Kain and asked him, "What do you mean?" He said, "That ain't no poem. That's just you ranting about the people in your neighborhood." I was so angry, I wanted to hurt Kain for coming down on my poem, but in time I realized he was right. Besides, when you brought a new poem in for approval and Nilaja didn't take his drums out of his duffel bag and start playing, something was wrong. While I was reading, Nilaja didn't even *look* at his drums. This rejection was a great lesson for me, even though at the time I didn't accept it very well.

Then I wrote a poem entitled, "New York, New York." Nilaja started playing right away, and it was accepted. Nilaja played a rhythm that sounded like people walking in the streets. He was so creative. The background chant of my poem was "New York, New York, The Big Apple." Everyone liked it including Kain. He had already written a poem entitled, "New York," but our poems were totally different. I remember at one performance someone yelled out "do New York" and when Kain started to do his poem, the person yelled out again, "No, do 'New York. New York The Big Apple.'" I could see Kain wasn't very pleased, but I was proud. These conflicts and competitive outbursts became ongoing.

Harlem, which is located in Manhattan, is an island surrounded by water: the East River is on the East Side, and the Hudson River is on the West Side. The Harlem River Drive runs parallel to the East River and becomes the FDR Drive when it gets into midtown Manhattan; and the Westside Highway runs parallel to the Hudson River. There were many days I would drive over the East River and meditate by the river, and watch the water flow. Sometimes, I'd just watch the big boats come in, which was a nice chill time for me. It's probably one of the reasons I didn't mind commuting from Queens, but Kain seemed to have a problem with me having a car.

He said to me one time, "You ain't no revolutionary driving to Harlem from Queens."

I quickly responded by saying, "You don't have to ride with me, you can take the train."

He didn't like that.

Then I said "That's right brother, I'm *driving* to the revolution. You can take the train, brother."

Even though we had this ongoing conflict, I learned a lot from Kain. Kain was responsible for The Last Poets having an aesthetic, a classy style that separated us from other groups. We performed at colleges and community events, while spending a lot of time performing on the weekends at the East Wind. None of us were connected to any of the known black concerns of the day, like the Black Panthers or The Nation of Islam.

We were independent.

And it was this independence that allowed us to stretch beyond ideologies and boundaries to try different things. Kain wrote and performed a one man, two act play entitled the "Epitaph of the Coagulated Trinity." It was done well and directed by this young Puerto Rican brother named Felipe Luciano, who had been attending most of the Last Poet shows at the East Wind.

Kain approached Felipe and asked him if he had any directing skills, and Felipe lied and said he did, so Kain had him direct his one man play. Felipe was this brown-skinned Puerto Rican brother who acknowledged his African roots. And since his father was an absentee dad, Felipe was willing to adopt Kain as his father. I guess he needed to fill that void.

I remember a really important show we had coming up at East Wind. The roster was Leroi Jones and the Spirit House Movers and Players, Sun Ra's Arkestra, and The Last Poets. This was the biggest show we ever had. At a meeting, David told us he could not be there because he was going on a field trip with his psychology class.

We couldn't believe it. This was an important show and David wasn't willing to cut class!

Kain said, "I'm going to tell you like the Jew, if you can't come on Monday don't come Tuesday." David decided to go anyhow, and there was Felipe, waiting in the wings. So Kain decided to make Felipe our third poet. He had a real thing about the trinity, everything in "threes." Because Felipe had been at many of our performances, he already knew most of our material, and he was also very smart and talented. But he fit in perfectly mainly because he could sing. Felipe and I could harmonize easily, and Kain loved it. It made him feel like a reverend with a back-up choir. I used to say Kain wanted to be like James Brown and Jesus Christ.

Instead of walking on water, he wanted to slide across the water like James Brown.

The weekend was a big success. The East Wind was packed for three straight nights. Felipe fit in like a hand in a glove.

Over the years, out of the seven poets who have been in the group, the combination of Kain, Felipe and myself was the strongest. When David came back, he found he had lost his spot to Felipe. He was disappointed, but he liked Felipe too. Now with a Puerto Rican in the group, we were crossing racial barriers.

We were bridging the gap and showing our connected heritage.

I remember we had this dream gig at Antioch College in Yellow Springs, Ohio. We stayed there almost a week. The black students had been given their own space, their own dormitory and auditorium. Back then blacks were making demands all around the country, and on college campuses especially. Sometimes you get what you want. We had a beautiful black time there. We were really something to reckon with during the sixties.

When Felipe first joined the group, he had no poetry. He wrote a poem that I quickly rejected entitled, "Faces in the Forest." I told him he was really writing about the Cuban revolution not the Black Power movement. I told him there is no forest here, we're dealing with the streets. Because of Felipe's brilliance he heard what I said, and wrote a superbly written poem entitled, "Hey Now." It was about the street gangs of the city getting together and fighting against the cops. *The poem was brilliant.*

My poetry was getting stronger. Kain was already there and now with Felipe, The Last Poets had become major players in the world of black revolutionary poetry. The birth of The Last Poets was complete. ■

CHAPTER 7

The Takeover of 125th Street and 7th Avenue

IN 1969 WE WERE ALL SO revolutionary. We heard Black Power and many of us wanted to be Black Power. We wore our Afros proudly, sometimes with the afro pick with the clenched fist stuck in it. We had our revolutionary apparel, the dashiki and the gele. Even though our dashikis weren't bullet proof nor were our Afros a weapon, we acted like they were.

I remember a group of sisters who called themselves The Harlem Committee for Self-defense. They were some of the most intelligent sisters I have ever met. We spent a lot of time arguing about Marxism and Leninism. I was a staunch Black Nationalist, so our arguments were heated.

The sisters had been doing research on the state government's land encroachment in Harlem, so they knew there were plans to build a state office building in the middle of Harlem. They knew when construction was suppose to start, and that July 1, 1969 was the target date. All of this was being decided without the consent of the Harlem community.

Gaye Todd, one of the members of the committee, could sing and play the guitar. She would sing the song,

"We don't need a state office building in Harlem. We need a high school." One of the other sisters would pass out flyers to let people know what was going on. Although Harlem has a very large population, there was no public high school in central Harlem. The only high school in West Harlem was Rice High School, which is a Catholic school. Most of the west Harlem residents are protestant, not Catholic. After they demolished the buildings that had been in that empty lot, it seemed like an ideal place for a high school. The sisters had done their homework, and they even had an architect's design of what the school would look like, but the government had other plans.

The bulldozers and the trucks would be there Monday morning to start construction, so a big demonstration was organized on June 30 that Sunday. The hope was that many of the people would be there in the morning of July 1 to stop the construction from getting started. We had the drummers playing, a big fire burning, and a lot of curious people on the site. The site was fenced in by the construction crew that was there to demolish the old buildings. There were two important spots housed in two of the demolished buildings; the African National Memorial Bookstore, and the Tree of Life Bookstore of Harlem. The African Memorial bookstore, which was owned and operated by Lewis H. Michaux, had been a treasure for years, and served as a gathering place and haven for students, intellectuals, writers and artists. You could find black books there that you never knew existed, and Mr. Michaux could tell you anything about those books, including the authors since he probably read each and every one of them.

The other spot was really an organic self-help center, more than a bookstore. The Tree was run by a brother named Kanya Vashon McGhee. Kanya and his assistant knew all about herbs, and how to use them to cure ailments. They made herbal teas that you could sample right there in the place. I've seen junkies come in and read a book, drink the herbal tea and in many cases wean themselves off of whatever medication they were on. The Tree had a comfortable lounge area where you could chill and read, and a safe haven where an addict could come in and kick their habit.

Both places had been on the ground floor of the two buildings that had already been demolished. *Safe havens, a space for wellness, a place that shelters knowledge, and community gathering spot were destroyed. A coincidence? I think not.*

The drums were playing. You could hear them blocks away. The fire was burning. One of the committee sisters, Marlena Franklin, asked me to buy some watermelons to lure even more people onto the site. Marlena was the never mentioned daughter of the actress Cicely Tyson (neither confirmed nor denied by Tyson). Marlena was smart, beautiful, and a chocolate delight. Along with Gaye and Marlena, there was also April Spriggs, a nurse at Harlem hospital, Charlotte Orange, and Juana Clarke. There were other sisters as well but these sisters made up the core group of the committee.

I remember one day a white woman wearing an African print dress appeared on the site. The sisters did not like this at all, more so because she was wearing an African print dress. When April saw her, she asked her why she was there. I don't know what she said, but the next thing we all saw was this white woman running off the site and down the street being chased by a bunch of sisters. A passing police car saw what was happening, and decided to intervene and help her get away.

I think a bunch of angry sisters is about scarier than a bunch of angry men.

The police officer stayed in his car, and opened up the back door so the woman could jump in, and then the car sped away. It was like a cartoon, watching the sisters chase this white woman off the site and down the block.

So, Marlena gave me some money and asked me to go to the Bronx Market and get as many watermelons as I could with the money. I went to the market and got 38 watermelons, but just before I drove off, I realized I could buy one more and put it on my lap. So now I had 39 watermelons. When I got back to the site with the melons, it looked like the sisters had performed magic. They created a makeshift table with cloth covering these two wide pieces of plywood, and by the time they finished slicing the watermelons, it looked like they had at least a thousand slices on display.

The watermelon was like bees to honey. The people came onto the site to get their free slice of melon. They also got literature about the takeover, and how they could help. It was a great demonstration, and I think the watermelon really set it off on a hot summer's day.

Some brothers had hooked up a speaker system using the street light for electricity. They had a microphone and that's where I was on the mic, talking to the people. Reinforcing what the leaflets said. We had a big circle going around the fire chanting known black chants of the day. Some of them were, "We love our sisters and brothers, We love our sisters and brothers, I say deep deep down down deep down in our souls." Another one was "Beep Beep, Bang Bang, Ungawa, Black Power," and "Who shall survive America? Very few niggers and no crackers at all!"

This was our verbal armor of the day. We were having revolutionary church out there.

This went on for hours. I remember I was supposed to be conducting a poetry workshop at the East Wind, and my guest was a very good poet from Atlanta, Georgia who was A.B Spellman. Since I wasn't there, he came to the site to do his poetry using the bullhorn. We were having a revolutionary good time. There was a cheese bus on the site left by the previous workers. Some overzealous brothers set it on fire. I didn't think it was a good idea, but the fire was raging. While the bus was burning some folks were chanting and acting like we were burning the system down.

I really didn't think it was such a good idea to burn up the bus, but it was done.

The demonstration lasted all night. The nocturnal nature of black folks became evident as the crowd grew larger throughout the night. We knew we had more than enough folks to stop the construction come morning. And when morning came, we weren't even tired, we were ready for the confrontation. In fact, there must have been at least a thousand people who had broke night and were ready for the confrontation, *but there was none.*

Summers in the sixties were considered riot season, so in order to prevent a riot, the powers that be decided to postpone the construction. I grabbed the mic and shouted, "This is reclamation site number one!" When the parks man came to hoist the American flag, we snatched it and hoisted the red, black and green flag in its place. We were declaring war.

Many of us felt at that moment the revolution was on.

I had everyone there stand in front of the flag pole and with a Black Power salute make a pledge to the red black and green. *"Red is for the blood we've shed. Black is for the people. Green is for the land we are reclaiming. This is Reclamation Site Number 1."*

Many of us were living on the site. We put together a makeshift shelter, and got a huge canvas to cover the burnt out bus. We had a speaker system on top of the bus and it was from there that I spoke to the people. I would tell them why we were there, and what they could do to support our efforts. We were surrounded by all the black cops that were on the force.

Many of our brothers and sisters were calling them "black pigs."

"Off the pig" was an expression we had been using for a while, but it referred mainly to white cops. Now that they had black cops they were called "pigs" too. I knew confronting and name calling the black cops was what the establishment wanted, to have us fighting against each other. I decided to flip it. Over the mic I told the sisters and brothers, *"Do not harass the 'Brothers in Blue.' They are still our brothers and they have a job to do."*

The very next morning, all of the cops were white. I guess my message was working. You could always hear me loud and clear, but you couldn't see me because I was inside the bus.

I had two magical brothers on my team: Tazz and Juice. Anything I needed, anything I wanted, they would get it for me. I told them we needed a way to communicate with each other quickly. We had brothers stationed on Lenox and 126th Street, and at Seventh and 125th Street, because we didn't want any surprises. If any of the brothers saw the police mobilizing and getting ready to vamp on us, we wanted to be ready.

I really don't know how Tazz and Juice did it, but they came back to the site with a box of new walkie talkies (it was rumored that they stole them from the precinct). *They don't call us the impossible people for nothing.* There was a lot of debris scattered across the site, so we cleaned it up and created a road that went the length of the land. We called the road "Liberation Road."

I remember one day the police captain came onto the site to speak to whoever was in charge. We had already predicted this, and had decided when they asked us who is in charge, we would all count to three then raise our hands. There were sixteen coordinators and we called ourselves the "community collision." The police captain was obviously frustrated, "I can't talk to all of you at one time." We said, "It's all of us or none of us."

The theory they were flirting with was; kill the head the body dies. *We were not having it.*

Everyday I continued my morning, afternoon and evening talks to the Harlem people. One day we were graced with the presence of Adam Clayton Powell Jr. He came to the site looking just like the stories we had heard about him, dressed to the nines with a pretty brown-skinned sister on each arm. He also had a cigar in his mouth and looked like the quintessential player's player, and walked with a swagger. As the congressman from Harlem, he got more laws passed than any politician in the history of America. The beauty of Adam was that he loved Harlem, and he looked out for the people of Harlem. When the anti-poverty programs started in the sixties, Adam made sure that Harlem got a big chunk of that money.

The money he got created jobs for almost all the residents of Harlem. There were many summer youth programs, where the young people could earn money. After all these years, I still feel honored and blessed that I had a chance to meet Adam in this lifetime. He walked around the site and checked out what we were doing. Then he walked up to me and asked me if I was in charge. I told him we had an entire committee that was in charge, and that I was just one of the coordinators.

"This is how you do it. Sometimes you gotta take direct action if you want to get the right results."

I felt even better now that "The Man" had endorsed our efforts. We all felt very good about that. He left soon after, telling us to keep it up, and we felt proud of ourselves.

I don't know where they came from, but we had very large pots that we used to cook food for the masses. The sisters made huge pots of chili and rice. We bought some paper plates, and the folks ate well. Some ate better than they did at home.

We were living in the rough because we were serious. One Sunday we got word that an elderly sister wanted to donate canned food, clothes and money. So I loaned my car to one of our brothers, and sent him to get the donations. It was a special day on the site because the Yoruba Society came to bless us with drums, chants and dancing. *We were being blessed by our ancestors and the Yoruba Gods.* A lot of us are not aware that the vast majority of us come from Yorubaland (the cultural region of the Yoruba people in West Africa) where we are eight million people strong. *So this celebration was like a real homecoming.*

Then all of a sudden a brother got on the mic and called my name frantically. He got my attention, but also the attention from everyone else. I went to the brother and he told me that the police had beaten up Robert, who I lent my car to, and impounded my car. The police gave Robert a concussion and broke his arm. And they never called an ambulance, they took him straight to jail. Someone said they thought he was me. They planted drugs and a gun in my glove compartment. I guess this was the ultimate setup. I had never dealt with drugs in my life, and I had my gun with me. So now I knew the cops were really trying to get rid of me because, I guess, my mouth was a little too big.

After a day or two they discovered that while the car was mine, they had the wrong man, and put out a warrant for my arrest. A few brothers came to me and said my being there would give the police a perfect excuse to take over the site, and that I had to get out of Harlem, so I left.

The takeover continued throughout the summer. Once the school year began, many of the young activists who were college students returned to school, which left a considerably smaller group at the site. Eventually, *they* pulled the red, black and green flag down, and put the American flag back up in itself. The committee took it down, again. Then *they* decided to cut the cord, but a young agile brother climbed the pole, and put our flag back up, and everyone cheered. The next thing *they* did was grease the pole, but that still didn't stop us. So finally, they took the flag pole down. And then one gray day in September the cops rolled in and took over the site.

Some people refused to leave and they were arrested. Since it was a much smaller group, it was relatively easy for the cops to take control. The very next day the bulldozers and the trucks arrived, and started excavating the land to construct the largest white phallic symbol in Harlem. It's still standing today, and its called The Harlem State Office Building. However, very few offices are occupied, and it's been like that for over forty years.■

CHAPTER 8

An Adventure in Morocco

JUDY COULD REALLY READ a map. She knew what the different colors represented, and knew how to follow those little lines. She would discover what mode of transportation we needed to take, and the time it took to get there.

We left New York City and landed in Madrid, Spain. We rented a car and drove around Madrid for a day or two. We visited Museo Nacional Del Prado, and some spectacular cathedrals. You could feel the class of Spain, and Madrid was just the beginning. Because of Judy's map skills, she figured we could drive at least three hundred miles a day, and see all that we needed to see from Madrid to Málaga.

The drive to Southern Spain was exciting and educational. We even stopped in Granada, Andalusia, and visited the Alhambra, the "Red One," a fortress initially built by the Moors in AD 889 that endures as a typical example of Muslim art in its final European stages. The Alhambra was special. It has hanging gardens, terrace farming, fabulous mosaics everywhere and water streaming down the banister of staircases high up on a hill so they could see who was coming.

We finally arrived at Málaga, which is located on the south shore of Spain along the Mediterranean Sea. Once we got there, we stayed in a very luxurious hotel called the Atlantic. It looked like a place only for the rich and famous. Judy, however, with the help of her sister Stephanie had discovered these vouchers that we could use as money for the hotel and food. Some of the exclusive places were on the voucher list, but I don't think many of them were ready to see two black folks from Harlem with them. They were accepted, but by some reluctantly.

I don't exactly remember what happened, but for some reason Judy and I were at odds with each other. So here we were in this grand hotel not sleeping together. She slept in the bed and I on the floor. In the morning we cleared the air and got back on track, and started on a new adventure. We were just across the sea from Africa and Judy had planned for us to go there.

"You see those little red lines here," Judy said, while pointing at the map.

I said, "Yes, I see them."

"Those lines represent a ferry that goes across the sea into North Africa!" she exclaimed. "If we drive further down to Algeciras, we can catch the ferry there. We can put the car on the boat and visit Morocco." The trip was already adventuresome, but now we're going to take it to another level. I was excited that we were going to explore both the European and African continents in one trip. The ancestors had truly blessed us.

I drove the car onto the ferry and we started our voyage across the Mediterranean Sea. The boat was rather full, and there were a lot of Muslims aboard—you could tell from their apparel. I stood along the railing of the boat and watched these big gray fish jump out of the water, like they were putting on a show. I don't know if they were dolphins, but they sure looked like them. I was really surprised when we went right pass the Rock of Gibraltar; I had read about it in school, and now to see it live was an experience. First of all I never knew people actually lived on the rock. There were houses there. I was surprised. Finally we arrived in Tangier, Morocco. I was ecstatic. This was my first time stepping on the continent of Africa. I think I even kissed the ground.

We were driving up to the building where you've got to do the paper work if you're a visitor, when a Puerto Rican looking brother came up to my window and said, "What's happening brother?" I was shocked. He sounded like he was from the Bronx, and how did he know I spoke English?

I smiled and asked, "What's up?"

Judy on the other hand got tight. She wasn't feeling him.

"Hey look brother, I can take care of your paperwork so you won't have to wait on the line," he said.

"We're not giving up our passports!" Judy exclaimed.

"I don't need your passport."

I looked at Judy like, why aren't you more trusting? The young man left, and in a few minutes he came back with the papers we needed.

"I know you just got here, and if you don't have a hotel I can take you to one that's nice and not expensive" he said.

"Sure," I responded. He got in the back of the car and led us through the streets of Tangier to this hotel that had a parking garage underneath it. I kept looking at Judy as if to say, "See, he's an angel." She wasn't buying it. I went up-stairs to check-in, thinking that Judy was close behind me, but it was only when the desk clerk asked me if I was alone that I discovered she wasn't there. So I excused myself and went to see where she was. Judy was at the bottom of the staircase and refused to come up.

"You can stay here. I am not," she said, emphatically. I went downstairs to see if I could convince her that everything was alright when I happened to look where I had parked the car, and there were three guys standing around like they were getting ready to break in. I yelled and they started running. Judy gave me that look that only a woman can give a man — that "I told you so" look. She saw it coming from the very beginning. I said nothing.

We got back in the car and started riding aimlessly through Tangier. It was evening, and in a short while it would be dark. I worried about where we would stay. We had money and a credit card so I figured we would find a place soon, because I just didn't trust myself to drive around the city at night.

You see, these streets, the flow of traffic, and the people didn't act like the folks back in New York. First of all, many of the people walked in the street alongside the cars. Just when I felt defeated, a kid on a motorcycle with a friend riding on the back pulled up alongside of my window and asked, "Amigo want to get high?"

I didn't say anything. I just looked at Judy. She said, "Yes," and the kid said, "Follow me."

So we followed him up this steep hill that gave us a perfect view of the city of Tangier. Then he gave us one of the most potent joints I've ever smoked. It was hash laced with tobacco. I don't smoke tobacco, but I figured I'd try to go along with the custom. Judy smoked cigarettes on occasion so she was good. The young man introduced himself as Jamel, and his friend Jalil, who was the son of a Moroccan rug manufacturer. Both of these kids were obviously rich and led a carefree life. Jamel asked me if we had a place to stay. I told him no. He offered his place. He said he lived in a big house with a lot of rooms. I looked at Judy and she did not object. The only problem now was getting down from this steep hill. Now that I had smoked that very potent hash, the hill looked even steeper and I was hesitant about driving. Jamel noticed and said, "Amigo I got it" He got behind the wheel and safely got us back to level ground.

We went to his house it was a villa on the second highest hill in Tangier after the Governor's house. It was obvious Jamel's family had money, they even had servants. Even though it was late when we arrived, we met his mother and the servant made us some mint tea, toasted some brown bread, and served it with jam and butter. Jamel's mother was beautiful. Her name was Margarita and she reminded me of Elizabeth Taylor because she had violet eyes. She was very friendly, and more importantly, she and Judy seemed to like each other from the start. Although Margarita didn't speak English as well as Jamel did, and French and Spanish wasn't Judy's strong point, they managed to communicate very well. Margarita provided us with a cozy room to sleep in, and the accommodation was wonderful.

Judy nor I realized at the time that Jamel told his mother we were teachers from America, and that we were going to help him finish his high school education. Jamel had been expelled from both the French and Moroccan schools, so he could only finish his education at the American academy in Tangier. I asked Jamel what was the problem with school, and he said, "Amigo, what can they teach me?" He had a point— he was very smart.

In the morning Hemido (the servant) offered to wash our clothes. Judy refused but I did not. I gave him everything that needed washing. Then I went to take a shower, which was right next to the swimming pool that was on the roof of the villa. So here I was taking a shower in broad daylight on top of a hill looking down at the city of Tangier. I could see everything, but no one could see me. The pool was designed with beautiful mosaics, surrounded by grape-vines. This was living. It was very surreal.

"Amigo," which is all Jamel ever called me. "If you want any hash just reach into any trophy and you'll find some there. I had noticed there were a lot of trophies in the house. I had noticed when we first arrived that the entire house was decorated with trophies. Jamel's father had been an equestrian champion of Morocco for ten years straight. Judy had discovered that Jamel's father was in jail for selling hash, and all of the family's assets were frozen. There were two Mercedes in the garage, but they didn't have gas. The servants remained in service figuring that they would be paid eventually.

Judy and I came at a time when Margarita needed it the most. She confided in Judy like they were old friends. Now I understood why Jamel wanted to use my car. I didn't really need the car. Being in the house was great and having an unlimited amount of hash was even greater. Judy went to play Bingo with Margarita and discovered more about their culture. She asked Margarita if she ever felt bad having to walk behind the men. She answered, "No, besides the men spit when they talk."

We had a wonderful time staying at the house. We ate well. I did some writing and reading, and acted like I was on a real vacation. Jamel had two younger sisters, Selena and Lela. Selena was the youngest, about eight years old. Lela was a teenager, and was fascinated by Judy's clothes and jewelry. Judy wore a lot of gold and onyx. I told Lela I had met her before I ever saw her. Lela spoke English very well so we could easily have a conversation. I told her my son

Oba had an imaginary friend and her name was Lela. She laughed and thought that was funny.

One day Margarita decided to visit her husband's parents in Ketama. So Margarita, Jamel, Judy and I packed into the car and started on our way. We made a stop in Tétouan. We discovered later that was the prison where Jamel's father was being held. Margarita got out, and we continued on to Ketama. We were riding through the countryside of Morocco, but there were issues. Every now and then I'd come across a boulder in the middle of the road that would cause me to slow down to go around it. When I'd slow down, some young kid would run up to the car trying to sell hash. I didn't realize we were riding through a marijuana forest. When Jamel realized I wasn't familiar with this practice, he told me he'd drive, and that he would stop the harassment. One time after we switched, a kid did run up to the car and Jamel said something in Arabic that made the kid run the other way. No one ever bothered us again.

We finally arrived at his grandparents' place. They had a big spread with a big house where they lived, and another house was being built on the property. The new house stuck out like a sore thumb. Everything on the property looked rustic, but the new house, which was more modern looking, was out-of-sync with its environment. Jamel said that the new house was being built for his grandparents. I told Judy now I understood why his father was in prison. Here in the middle of nowhere they were building a palatial mansion.

We walked around the land and I soon realized we were on a marijuana farm. I asked Jamel why his family didn't grow any vegetables. He told me they tried, but marijuana took over. He said even after the government burned down the farm a year ago, the marijuana came back even stronger the next year. I walked on more marijuana than I could ever smoke in my lifetime. There were young kids with these little black balls that looked like the hand balls you play with when you play paddle ball. They were actually hash balls and the kids were concentrating the hash for sale.

We checked out the new house being built. It was something special. The rooms were large and there were beautiful mosaics on the walls. It had such a peaceful vibe. I guess I was high, but I decided to take a nap right there. After awhile we went back to the main house where I met four young men, one of whom was Jamel's brother Faisal. They had a young bull that they were trying to take to a certain area, but the animal was resisting. I was curious and went outside to see what they were trying to do with it.

Judy hung out with the women who were washing clothes in a pond. Once again Judy's jewelry stood out. There was this one woman who was fixated on Judy's onyx. The woman made Judy a little nervous, but she soon realized the woman was fascinated by the black stones.

In the meantime, I decided to follow the men with the bull. They came to a spot and turned the bull on his side then held him down. Jamel's grandfather came with a long shinny knife, and with one or two strokes decapitated the bull. I was shocked. I had never seen anything like this before. After he severed the head from the body, the young men released the bull and to my amazement, the eye was opening and closing and the headless body struggled to get on its feet. It only took a few steps but the headless bull was coming towards me. *I was shook.*

I later found out that this is how kosher meat was made. When you slit the throat, the blood comes out like a fountain thereby cleansing the meat.

Later on that day when I got good and hungry, one of the ladies brought me some soup with little round potatoes. The soup was made from the bull's flesh. I couldn't even eat it. As a matter of fact, I didn't eat any meat for at least a month after that.

Judy and I sat in the house waiting for Jamel to return with the car when it started to rain. The roof of the old house was made of tin, and when the rain hit against it, it sounded like bullets being shot. Then we noticed that all the animals outside, like the horses and the cows were brought into the house to get out of the rain. This was a lifestyle I knew nothing about.

I sat there wishing Jamel would soon return so we could go back to Tangier. *My Ketama experience was now over the top.*

He finally returned. We said our goodbyes and started back. On the way back we did not stop in Tétouan to pick up Margarita, but went straight to Tangier, but I had an experience there that I would never forget.

Judy and I were in Tangier for over a week, but now it was time for us to return to Spain, and catch our flight back to the United States. Because Lela was infatuated with Judy's shoes and jewelry, Judy gave her a bracelet and a pair of shoes that she had already stretched out because she wore them in Judy's absence. The only problem was the car wasn't there. Jamel had used it more than I did, but I felt it was a good trade-off because we were staying in his house, but I didn't like the idea of not knowing when he would return. On this particular day, I was feeling a little uneasy. Judy and I needed to make moves to go home. I asked his brother Faisal, and he told me Jamal was probably hanging out at Club Med.

Jamel was only eighteen. No one under twenty-one was permitted there, but Jamel was no average eighteen year old. Since Jamel's father was in prison, he now conducted the family's hash business, and it was easy to see why. Jamal was handsome, and he had a lot of charm. He spoke at least seven languages, and he had an endearing personality. *But I needed the car back so we could go home, so I took a taxi to Club Med.*

I asked the security guard if he saw a young man in a beige Fiesta. The security guard said, "Jamel is inside at the bar." I went to the bar and there he was, with a woman sitting on both sides. One woman spoke French, the other Spanish, and Jamel was playing them both at the same time. I interrupted this comedy of errors and told Jamal we had to get back so we left.

When we returned to the house we said our goodbyes to the family and the servants. Judy and Margarita hugged each other like old friends. This wild but wonderful adventure was coming to an end, and Margarita looked rather sad that we were leaving. Jamel asked me if I thought he could be a Hollywood actor like James Dean. I told him he could be better than him. We all hugged each other one more time, and then Judy and I took off to the ferry that would travel across the Strait of Gibraltar to Spain. *Of course, we weren't off the hook, yet.*

I realized when we got in the car I needed gas. I had less than a quarter of a tank left and I knew that would not be enough to get us to Málaga. I figured once we arrived in Spain, I would get some gas and we would be alright. The only problem was I had spent all of my money buying food for the house while we were there. I knew Judy had a credit card, but when she checked her purse she didn't have it. Then she remembered—she left it at the hotel desk in Málaga. So here we were, on a boat back to Spain with no money, no credit card, and very little gas in the car. We were also getting a little hungry as we watched people eating sandwiches and drinking. *We didn't have a clue as to how we would rectify the situation.*

Both of us sat there without saying a word, but it seemed like both of us were meditating on the same thing. Then all of a sudden, this tall attractive white woman walked up to us and asked, "Do you speak English?" I was so surprised. I almost choked on my answer when I said, "Yes, we do."

"My name is Ingrid, and I've been held on this boat for ten hours because I left my passport in Spain," she said. "Do you have a car?"

I said, "Yes, we do, but it has very little gas."

"Well I have money to buy gas if you could take me to get my passport." Then she pulled out enough money to choke a horse. *Our angel has arrived, I thought to myself.*

When we arrived in Spain, I was so happy I decided to smoke a hash joint. I wasn't even thinking about the customs agent in Spain. All the cars were lined to go to customs inspector. When I realized that we had to go through inspection, I quickly put the joint out and opened the windows to get the smoke out of the car. After I got the fumes out, I rolled the windows back up. I was still a little worried because I knew I had hash on me packaged by Jamel. When the agent came to the window, there was a big German Shepard by his side. I got nervous. In Spanish the agent told me to open the door. I acted like I didn't understand what he was saying. Then he started banging on top of the car with his stick. I opened the door and the dog put his face in the car. I could actually feel his chin on my lap. The hash was right there in my pocket. I just knew I was busted. The dog did nothing. Then the agent said we could go. I was relieved. I then asked Ingrid what was the dog suppose to do if he smelled hash. Ingrid said, "They bark." When we were safely away from the gate, I pulled out the hash and gave it to Ingrid and asked her, "What is this?" She said, "This is hash alright, but it's been laced. If you lace the hash with something like cinnamon, the dog can't smell it."

"I see Jamel knows all the tricks."

We went to a gas station and I got a full tank. Then we went to Torremolinos, a little town en route to Málaga. This is where Ingrid left her passport. Then Ingrid took us to an all night place to eat, and we ate like it was Thanksgiving. After we ate we went to Málaga and got Judy's credit card. Ingrid said she was not going to take the ferry back to Morocco; she was going to fly to Casablanca. Judy and I had a flight to New York the next day. So we decided to spend the night at the airport. Ingrid slept inside the terminal, and Judy and I slept in the car.

The adventure was winding down and we had been angels for each other. A Belgium woman and two African-Americans working together. Humanity was alive and well. I had not written anything during the Moroccan trip, but I told Judy I was definitely going to try and capture the adventure in a poem or a song. When I got home, I wrote a song entitled "Jamelintine," and it's probably one of the best story songs I've ever written. ■

CHAPTER 9

Scarecrow

NOT TOO LONG AGO in a rice village in West Africa lived a special girl named Oduwa. When she was born, there was a great celebration because she was the first child of a new union.

It became apparent after a while that she was not going to be so pleasing to the eye. You couldn't look at her and say, "Oh, you have such a pretty baby." Oduwa was not pretty, but her mother and father loved her just the same.

When she started going to school, some of the children would tease her about her looks. She tried not to let it bother her, but it did. Oduwa didn't look like her mother or father; let's just say she had her own "look."

One day, when Oduwa was very young, the village chiefs came to her house to ask her parents to use Oduwa as a human scarecrow to shoo away the crows that would come to feed off of the rice paddies. Her mother cried and protested, "You want to use my daughter as a human scarecrow?" She felt this was an insult and an embarrassment to Oduwa and the family.

The village chiefs told them that they would be greatly compensated. At first, they said no, but then after discussing it and thinking about how they could spend the money, they decided to go along with it. Still, her mother feared this could scar Oduwa for life, and she would never feel good about herself. Her father felt the same way, but they both agreed that more cowrie shells (a form of money they used at that time) they had, the more things they could buy at the market. Oduwa was an obedient child, so she did what she was told.

Every morning just before dawn Oduwa would go into the fields to shoo away the crows so they wouldn't eat the rice. This caused her to get teased even more by the children at school. They would point at her and say, "Scarecrow, scarecrow, Oduwa's a scarecrow!" They even created a game of tag, and if you got tagged then you were now the scarecrow. Oduwa never played the game. What they didn't know was that Oduwa never really shooed the crows away from the rice paddies. She would sing and dance all around the field, and the birds were so enchanted they never touched the rice.

Oduwa seemed to enjoy performing for the birds. She was able to create her own little world where she entertained Mother Nature, and really didn't care what the other children said. This went on for quite a while. Her mother was still very distraught over her daughter's job, but she noticed it didn't seem to bother Oduwa.

"You don't mind scaring the birds away, Oduwa?" her mother asked.

"No I don't mind momma."

"I hear that the children tease you at school about it."

"It doesn't bother me," she'd say.

It had to affect her in some way, her mother thought. Her mother didn't know what she was really doing out in the fields at five o'clock in the morning, but because of

Oduwa, her father was able to buy new things for the house and for Oduwa and his wife, so she didn't really ask.

One day when Oduwa was about fourteen years old, her father came home with this beautiful fabric he had bought while visiting the city. He gave some to his wife and Oduwa. Oduwa loved it. It was purple and gold, and looked like something only royalty would wear.

There was a big drum and dance festival coming up this year, and it was going to be held right there in Oduwa's village. She had an idea of making something special for this occasion. She knew everyone would be there and for some reason, she felt this was going to be a very special day for her. Oduwa made a beautiful dress.

When her mother saw it she exclaimed, "This is such a beautiful dress!"

"I thought I might wear it at the festival," Oduwa said.

"I think that's a wonderful idea. You'll be the talk of the village. They will all admire you. You did a great job."

Her mother gave her a big hug and kiss, and then left her standing there with a big smile on her face.

Oduwa could not wait for the day to arrive. The birds seemed to know it as well. It appeared that the birds were coming to the fields but not to eat the rice, but to hear Oduwa sing and watch her dance. Her audience had grown so big that even the trees seemed to be affected by her movements.

On the day of the festival Oduwa woke up feeling bright and cheerful. She knew today was going to be a special day. The whole village was abuzz. Everyone was getting ready. Every now and then you could hear a drum or a kora. This was a day when all the neighboring villages would get together and celebrate being alive and well, and ask the Gods to protect them and help them prosper for another year.

People were excited especially the children. This would be an opportunity for some to fall in love. Oduwa didn't know why but she too thought that today would be a major turning point in her life. After she completed all of her chores, she took an herbal bath then got dressed. While she was putting the dress on she could feel something happening inside like she was being transformed. She loved the dress and thought it was just her imagination that made her feel like that. Once she finished dressing she couldn't stop admiring herself in the mirror.

"I'm just dreaming," she said to herself. Her mother entered her room.

"Oh my God. You look so beautiful Oduwa!" Her mother was amazed.

Oduwa still had the same face but for some reason she didn't look the same. She looked like someone else. "I feel beautiful momma," she replied.

"Wait until they see you today. They will not call you scarecrow today, that's for sure." They embraced and smiled at each other like they both knew this was a precious moment.

In the background you could hear the drums. They were coming from everywhere, from the villages close by and even far away. You could feel the excitement in the air as the drums got louder and louder. Oduwa's father said, "We better go so we can get good seats. You know it's going to get crowded right away."

When Oduwa appeared he too was struck by her beauty. "My, my, you look different. I mean you look great. Wow! what did you do? That dress is beautiful and you look beautiful in it."

"You bought the material poppa I just made a dress but thank you for the compliment." He gave her a big hug, then just stared at her in admiration. "Well let's go to the festival, and let the world see my daughter," he smiled.

On their way to the festival, they would acknowledge those they saw, and each person would do a double take when they saw Oduwa. A young boy even yelled out. "Is that Oduwa?"

"Yes that is Oduwa," her mother said.

The crowd was assembling. Oduwa's father found a good spot right in the middle of the performance area, close enough to touch the drummers. The drums were going nonstop. Oduwa was happy, very happy.

A number of her classmates came up to her and said, "You look pretty Oduwa." She just smiled and said, "Thank you," in a very cordial way. Oduwa knew something was about to happen. She didn't know exactly what but she could feel it surging in her blood.

Something big was going to happen.

The village priest blessed the occasion and the festival began. The drumming was exceptional. Everyone was feeling them. One of the elders who was said to be over a hundred years old started little movements with his body to the rhythm of the drums. Everyone was moving, you couldn't help it the drums were intoxicating. Oduwa's head started spinning. She too was moving to the rhythm of the drums, but it was also having a very deep effect on her. She started transforming right there in front of the huge crowd.

Oduwa was becoming possessed.

Her mother noticed it right away and went to her. When she put her arms around her shoulders Oduwa broke loose and started dancing. She danced like no one had ever seen before. At times it appeared as if her feet never touched the ground. She would turn and spin, jump and fly all over the arena. Everyone was astonished. Oduwa was truly possessed.

She had a look of confidence that emitted a majestic beauty that radiated strength, passion and conviction that no one had ever seen. It was like she ascended and became a living God right there before the eyes of everyone

She danced and danced and the drummers were compelled to play just for her. The people started chanting her name, and she continued to dance. No one knows how long she danced. It was clear no one could follow Oduwa, and she never seemed to tire.

After a while Oduwa stopped and fell to the ground. Everyone rushed towards her. The priest made them get back and give her space. Her eyes were rolling back into her head and her body was trembling. The head priest said something and rang a little bell, and Oduwa came out of it. She went back to who she was before she started dancing.

"What happened?" she asked, wondering why she was on the ground with people standing around her.

"You blessed us with your gift," the priest said.

Her mother came to her and held her in her arms with tears streaming down her face. "The Gods did not forsake us. My child is a blessing. Thank you, Orishas, thank you," her mother testified.

Oduwa's father was rejoicing as well. Everyone in the village came up to him to congratulate him for having a special child. The festival continued, and throughout the rest of the day all everyone could talk about was Oduwa dancing and how they had never seen anything like it before.

From that moment on whenever Oduwa was seen the person would prostrate in front of her, and ask for a blessing. Overnight, she became a demigod. She was told many times by her family and friends that what she did that day, and just how unbelievable it was to witnessed it.

Oduwa, realizing that she had this gift, shared it with others. She even started a dance company right there in her village. When they traveled to other villages to perform, they were very much appreciated. Oduwa the scarecrow was long forgotten.

Oduwa had transformed from an ugly little bird into a beautiful swan.

Her story became legendary and she became one of the most famous dancers in the world with a dance troupe that was very well known. Even though Oduwa wasn't there to entertain the birds, they still didn't eat from the rice paddies. It was like it was out of respect for the many years they watched her dance. ∎

CHAPTER 10

Stuck in Abidjan, Côte d'Ivoire

THE IVORY COAST (CÔTE D'IVOIRE) IS BEAUTIFUL. The truth is, the entire West Coast of Africa is beautiful. I had received a fellowship from Columbia University, along with the opportunity to get a graduate degree, they give you money to live off of. There was enough money for me to pay my rent, and do something special like go to Africa.

Judy was my travel agent besides being my lady. She knew how to hook up a trip. She loved maps, and she was an avid reader. We never went anywhere without everything being prearranged. Because she had an American Express Gold Card, we knew money was not an issue. However, this was the one time I had the money to finance the entire trip. I was so proud of myself. The plan was to go to four African countries; Togo, Mali, the Ivory Coast and Senegal.

This story begins in the capital of the Ivory Coast Abidjan. When we arrived, we had not secured a place to stay. We rented a car, and figured we'd find something suitable since we had planned to only be there for three days. Then we would be off to Lomé, the capital of Togo. After looking around and not finding something we liked, I told Judy we should go big. She had told me about the Hotel Le'voire but it was very expensive. Since I had money, I decided we should splurge. Judy liked the idea and started calling me "Money Bags." It was a super five star hotel. It was probably the crown jewel of hotels in the country. It was really laid out with the beach right across the street. The architecture was special, the colors appealing, and the furniture had a modern African flavor. It was the kind of place where you knew you were on a grand vacation.

I had made a previous connection to go to the radio station for an interview. Being a famous poet from America has offered me some advantages that others may not have, but I rarely used that status because I prefer keeping a low profile. The radio interview went well, and I took pictures with everyone there. During this time I met a very nice brother, Emmett, from Detroit who was a musician in the studio band. We exchanged numbers, and I invited him to my house if he ever came to New York. At the time I didn't know who his wife was, but he said they would be in New York that coming summer.

We had been in the Ivory Coast for three days. We saw a lot, and enjoyed the time spent there. Then we moved onto our next country, which was Togo. Judy and I were up and out early. Emmett offered to take us to the airport. I had returned the rental car, so it was perfect to be offered a ride. When we got to the airport, instead of dropping us off, Emmett remained close by. We got on line to check in, and when we got to the counter, the agent she said there were no more seats available. She explained that they had overbooked. Judy and I had heard that one could get stuck in Africa, but we didn't think it would happen to us. Emmett suggested we spend the night at his home, and catch the plane tomorrow morning. We confirmed our seats for tomorrow's flight and went with Emmett to his house. *It was a villa.*

I don't even know how many rooms it had but it was big. It was also a dance school. We met his wife, Rose Marie Giraud, a world famous dancer. We sat in this huge living room. There were over thirty young people living there getting their basic education, and dance instructions. The young people did all the cooking and cleaning. The only room they were not allowed in except to clean it was the living room.

Judy and I had not eaten, and we could smell something good coming from the kitchen. Sister Rose told us we were going to have some chicken cooked in peanut sauce, a West African dish. I couldn't wait, I was really hungry. While we waited for the food, we talked about what she did with the young people, and how their parents would see them rehearse and visit them on the weekends. She had turned her home into a boarding school for young dancers. She also brought her students to America every spring to participate in DanceAfrica, a big event at Brooklyn Academy of Music (BAM). DanceAfrica was founded by Chuck Davis, who had come to Africa and studied under Sister Rose. *We live in a small world.*

After a while the food was brought out. *I was ready.* A young teenage girl brought out this big pot of rice. I had never seen a pot that big before, and it was half full with rice. Sister Rose looked in the pot, and a scowl appeared on her face.

"What is this?" she exclaimed. Then she reached her hand inside and grabbed a handful of rice and said, "This is not rice."

Then she threw the rice back in the pot and shouted, "Do it over!" The young girl was visibly upset but very obedient. She quickly took the pot away.

I was a bit disappointed because even though the rice was a little gummy, it was still edible to me since *I was hungry.*

"The rice must be cooked right. I come from a rice village, and you don't serve rice like that!"

I wanted to say that I could have eaten it with the peanut sauce, and would have been very happy, but Rose was adamant about the rice where every grain stood alone. I understood what she meant, but it didn't really matter to me. Then she told the story of her youth back in the village where she was raised. When Sister Rose was born, she wasn't considered a pretty baby. As a matter of fact, she was seen as an ugly duckling. Because of her looks, the village chief asked her family to let her scare away the crows from the rice paddies when she got a little older. They were told that they would be compensated for their daughter's services. Sister Rose's mother worried about her self-esteem being used as a human scare crow. The village was known for producing rice, but often the crows would eat up half of the would be profits.

It was hard but after much debate and discussion her family agreed that she would do it. As a little girl she would go out into the rice paddies at daybreak, and scare all the crows away. The village prospered greatly from this and Sister Rose's family was handsomely compensated. The ridicule that Sister Rose had to face by the other children didn't seem to bother her. She endured this until it was discovered that she had a gift for dancing. Once her gift was revealed they treated her like a deity. She then went on to become a world famous dancer. This is why the rice had to be done right.

Judy and I were fascinated by her story and understood where she was coming from. When the young girl brought the rice back it was perfect. We ate well. We were given a little room to sleep in and in the morning we went back to the airport and caught a plane to Togo. ■

CHAPTER 11

A Fishing Tale

BARBADOS IS A BEAUTIFUL ISLAND of palm trees and flowers, turquoise blue water and hot sun with a sweet breeze that keeps you cool. Barbados is also the home of the flying fish, so Judy and I decided to stay in a guest house instead of a hotel. Being in a guest house gives you more access to the people and the culture. Judy and I liked to be with the people, and we enjoyed learning about the place we were visiting first hand.

Ms. Rydell was the owner of the guest house. She was a heavy set light-skinned woman who you could see was an eye catcher some years ago. In fact, she had suitors even now. The house was quaint, and our space was very cozy. It was near a paradise of a beach where the water was as gentle as an adult pool made for swimming.

We normally rent a car right at the airport, but this time we waited and took a taxi or public transportation. I remember getting a bus at the depot in Bridgetown. I was fascinated by the African flavor I saw emanate from the people. Just like on the Ivory Coast, many of the women still walk carrying something on their head. The bus we got on was crowded, and there was this lady with a big bundle perfectly balanced on her head. The people were standing back to back. There was this other woman right behind me, and we were rubbing butt cheeks. I wondered if she was aware of this. So I turned to look at her and she smiled.

Barbados has a reputation for having the highest literacy rate of all the other islands. They're very proud of that, but sometimes arrogance comes with intelligence. We were in town during the Mardi Gras Festival, and a man who looked homeless approached me and asked for a quarter. It was festival time and I was feeling very good so I reached into my pocket and pulled out a dollar and handed it to him. He wouldn't take it. He angrily said to me, "I asked you for a quarter!" I was surprised. I just knew he'd be happy getting seventy-five cents more than what he asked for, but he wasn't.

It was this and other encounters that prompted me to write two songs while we were in Barbados, just because the place and the people lent itself to songs.

I had heard about the flying fish, but I had never seen one. Then one morning, when Judy and I were having a swim; I saw one, then two. Their fins were like little propellers, and they hovered about a foot or two above the water, then they went back into the water.

It always amazes me to see such wonderful things Mother Nature has created. Her creativity is unmatched.

Flying fish is so popular in Barbados that it has become a major export. They have packages of frozen flying fish that tourists can buy and bring back to the states. After tasting it, I understood the appeal. Flying fish has the same texture and taste of whiting, which is a popular fish among black folks in America. So Judy and I decided for the first time on a trip to hang out with some fishermen. Ms. Rydell told us that German and Bucker were two of the most well-known fishermen in the province of Christ Church, but if we wanted to go out with them, we'd have to get up very early in the morning. Getting up early was never a problem for either Judy or me, because we were both early risers anyway, so we made plans for our fishing adventure the next day.

That morning we got up at dawn. Ms. Rydell fixed breakfast for us, and then we went to the dock where the boats were docked. You could tell right away German and Bucker were two serious fishermen. German was a little older than Bucker, but they seemed to work well together, getting the gear and the boat ready for work. Neither had a problem with us coming with them. As a matter of fact, they seemed to like the idea of having company. It wasn't a big fishing boat, but it was big enough that it had a chair and a holder for the fishing rod in the arm. I sat in the chair imagining I was a fisherman for a day. German steered the boat while Bucker prepared the nets for catching fish. I was excited, anticipating a wonderful day of fishing in the Caribbean Sea. The sun wasn't at its peak yet, but you could feel it.

As we pulled away from the shore, the island of Barbados got smaller and smaller, and the ocean seemed vast and endless. The waves were a bit choppy, which made the boat rock a bit, but it didn't seem to affect Bucker, who walked around the boat and on top of the cabin like a tightrope walker with perfect balance. Judy and I held on to whatever was near us to steady ourselves.

There was hardly anything said between the two men, and when they did speak, they spoke in a dialect I couldn't understand. It's a whole different world being out at sea. After a while we didn't see any land at all and the color of the water went from a beautiful turquoise blue to almost black. It's rather mysterious because all you see is water. All you hear is the engine of the boat, and the splash of the water. It's also very peaceful and meditative. There was only one problem, we weren't catching any fish.

Judy and I were also getting very hungry. It must have been high noon because the sun was scorching. I had to give up sitting in the chair to lay down on the deck because I thought I was going to have a sun stroke. I kept looking at the fishing rod in the arm of the chair.

No tug on it at all. Nothing was biting.

Bucker was mixing something up in a little bowl. When I looked at it, it looked like tuna fish. Great, I thought, we're going to eat. He also had a little package of unsalted crackers. He shared this with Judy and me. We were very happy to get something to eat, but when we tasted it, it was not tuna fish as we thought. We couldn't figure out what it was but it tasted horrible. When Bucker wasn't watching, we threw it in the ocean. *I was hoping maybe it would attract some fish.*

We spent all day with German and Bucker out at sea, but we didn't catch a single fish.

You could tell they were not happy, and I immediately felt their bad luck was caused by our presence. It was evening when we got back to Christ Church. The sun was going down and many people were coming home from work. I don't even think we said goodbye to our escorts.

The word got out around town right away.

"Don't let those Americans on your boat. You won't catch any fish."

I felt bad and took most of the weight because I'm a Pisces, and I figured the fish knew a big fish was already on the boat and they were not going to join me. Judy and I laughed about it and said we gave the fish a reprieve to live another day.

I remember a few years later we ran into Danny Glover in Senegal, and he invited me to go Barracuda fishing with him. I quickly refused, thinking about the experience I had in Barbados. Judy and I never went on a fishing adventure again. ■

CHAPTER 12

A Last Poet in Senegal

IN DECEMBER 2012, I had the wonderful opportunity to visit Senegal in West Africa. My trip was sponsored by the American Embassy. Tony Vacca and his World Rhythms Ensemble had a hand in organizing the event, and I went with a group of artists, storytellers, poets and musicians to meet with the Hip Hop Academy in Dakar, Senegal about creating future joint programming with American and African artists.

I remember after completing a series of meetings, and a few of the artists and I performed. It was an insightful trip and I looked forward to working with the Hip Hop Academy on future projects.

Any time I take a trip to Dakar, I always make time to go to Gorée, the place where Africans were imprisoned until they were put on the slave ships, to think, reflect and honor my ancestors.

MY LADY AND I had visited Dakar, Senegal some years earlier. The strength, the beauty, the creativity, and the warmth of the people was impressive. Just to be in the Motherland was a joy and a dream come true.

We stayed at the Savana Jardin-Hotel Dakar, a five star hotel overlooking the island of Gorée. When we took the twenty minute ferry ride to Gorée, Judy and I immediately noticed the beautiful historical architecture, a testament to the four European nations that controlled the island at various points throughout history. When we arrived on the island, we visited the museum, The House of Slaves (Maison des Esclaves), that memorializes the final exit point of the slaves from Africa, and the Door of No Return, the last steps the Africans took out of their country. Gorée is not unique; depots like this one have dotted the entire coast of West Africa, transporting millions of slaves across the Atlantic. Ironically, the island is tranquil. Without cars or roads, Gorée preserves a charming ambiance with faded buildings revealing its European colonial history. But beneath its quaint façade, the island hides a brutal history.

When Judy and I arrived on the island, we explored The House of Slaves, and imagined the horror our ancestors went through. We stood in the dungeons where the Africans were warehoused. As many as thirty people, chained and shackled, one against another, would sit in an 8-square-foot cell with only a small slit of window facing outward.

Once a day, they were fed and allowed to attend to their needs, but still the house was overrun with disease. They were naked, except for a piece of cloth around their waists. They were put in a long narrow cell used for them to lie on the floor, one against the other. The children were separated from their mothers. Their mothers were across the courtyard, likely unable to hear their children cry. They were more than likely separated from men for the pleasure of the traders. The rebellious Africans were locked up in an oppressive, small cubicle under the stairs; while they sipped seawater through the holes to step up dehydration.

Being on that island with the knowledge of what had transpired was heart wrenching.

Standing in those cells plunged into darkness, I blinked, then squinted. A few seconds later it all sunk in. I can barely stave off the throat-tightening panic of claustrophobia, the overwhelming sadness. This dungeon wasn't even fit for a dog to live in.

After the waiting period, the slaves would be taken out of the cells, stripped naked and gathered in the courtyard so that the buyers and traders could observe the slaves while negotiating prices.

They were treated like merchandise.

The selected slaves would then be taken from the courtyard through the corridor to the Door of No Return where there would be a ship waiting to take them away. The most haunting thing about this place is that it is the moment of farewell—a final goodbye to a place they will never see again. Unable to cope with the long and traumatic journey, some Africans chose to kill themselves rather than be taken to some unknown fate, hoping death would return them home. They say the sharks would be waiting for their bodies to fall into the ocean, sometimes following ships out to sea for the bodies the ship's crew would throw overboard that threatened their cargo. We could feel the horror our ancestors went through as they took their final steps from their homeland onto slave ships that, if they managed to survive the journey, brought them to a new world.

While historians differ on how many African slaves were actually held in this building, as well as the relative importance of Gorée Island as a point on the transatlantic slave trade, *it really doesn't matter.* Numbers, figures, counts—quantification has a limit on what it can impress. It seems to me the wide gulf between the myth of the door and its reality may actually be, in itself, a revealing symbol of our relationship to this dark chapter in world history. Perhaps it's a twinge of denial.

Was it millions? Was it thousands? Does it matter?

What Judy and I felt at Gorée Island's famous pink-walled building is the haunting legacy and ineffable memory of human cargo being shipped to America. The memory of a people taken against their will that were hunted, captured, shackled, and treated like animals to be shipped like cargo to a foreign land to become some white man's property to do with as he pleased.

Human cargo.

The ghosts of our ancestors.

As I stood in the Door of No Return looking out onto the vast ocean, which is all any of the Africans could see from their dungeons, it was easy for me to imagine what they imagined: Home would become a distant memory. The mystery of what was on the other side, and what new horrors lay ahead. *Should I go, or should I die?*

I have been on the island several times since my first trip with Judy, and each time I always feel the pain my ancestors endured. But these trips also made me realize just how strong and resilient we are as a people. No one in the history of the world was ever stripped of their name, language and culture like we were. Gorée has become a symbol for the Diaspora, a place that urges us all to pause and remember the suffering that millions of slaves endured during the transatlantic slave trade. It exists as a reminder of what we've been through and how we came to America. As we visit places like Gorée Island, we shouldn't only remember the past, we should also be moved to action in the present.

IN 2014 I RETURNED TO SENEGAL. This trip was sponsored by a young man named Malaal, who runs a Hip Hop Academy in the suburbs of Dakar. I didn't realize that the American Embassy was actually funding this project. Apparently, because of the global appeal of hip hop, Americans had decided to use hip hop as an ambassador of sorts to establish a relationship with the country.

Malaal is into conscious hip hop, and is diametrically opposed to hip hop that uses the word "nigger," and makes videos of sisters shaking their behinds. The hip hop community there decided to have a hip hop conference in Gorée, so it was no coincidence that he brought me there to highlight conscious hip hop and poetry, since it's what I believe in and represent.

Since The Last Poets are regarded as the precursors of hip hop, the group is very much revered in Senegal. During the conference I wanted to set the record straight about The Last Poets. In our earlier poetry we used the word "nigger" a lot because we wanted black people to stop being niggers and be "Black." Somehow along the way the message got lost, and the term "nigger" became the most popular character for the hip hop community to use. I explained to the audience we were not giving that word a pass. I even got some of the brothers to erase the word from the walls of the Hip Hop Academy.

I was still learning Wolof, a native language of Senegal, but I could speak a little French. So at this huge Hip Hop Conference I said in French, *"Tu n'es pas Nigger, Tu es African* (You're not Nigger, you're African)." I kept saying it until the crowd repeated it. I was told that the young people were listening to me because they had dubbed me as the "Daddy Rapper."

At the end of the conference, we took a trip to Gorée, where I received a Citizen of Gorée Citation, and some apparel gifts from one of the hip hop groups, The Gobi System. I remember standing there in Gorée, and breaking down just thinking about the horrors my ancestors went through. I also spent time talking with the mayor of Gorée for the remainder of my visit.

Gorée, the place where our ancestors were imprisoned until they were put on the slave ships.

SENEGAL OFFERS A LOT of cultural differences. I immensely enjoyed immensely both the music and the food. Eating with the people in Senegal is a completely different experience. Everyone eats from the same platter, and your utensil is your right hand. In many cases, the mattress is on the floor and sometimes you have to use a bucket of water to flush the toilet. Coming from America, many of us take for granted certain amenities like toilet paper. You may have to bring your own when you visit Senegal unless, of course, you stay in a five star hotel. All of my trips to Senegal have been rewarding, very different each time, but always rewarding. I marvel at the creativity, the resilience and the beauty of African people. And each time I come to Senegal, it reinforces my pride in my race and the Motherland. ■

CHAPTER 13

A Legend on the Harlem Courts

WHEN HE WAS BORN no one had any idea who he was going to become and what he was going to do. He was a slightly built child, a few inches taller than the average child his age, but his magic wouldn't reveal itself until he was in the sixth grade. Even though he was slight of build, he had what they call the "hood hops," because he could jump up and take a quarter off the top of the backboard. His name was Joseph Riggins.

When he was twelve, he would play in the park with the big boys. It seemed he could get his shot off on anyone. If the defense was tight, he jumped so high when he made the shot, it was almost impossible to block it. Besides his phenomenal jumping ability, he was deceptively quick. You could be guarding him real close when all of a sudden, he would appear alongside you up in the air, ready to throw it down. He was really a marvel to see.

At sixteen, he was labeled one of the princes of the game, and they nicknamed him Supreme, and he tried to live up to it in everything he did.

I remember one summer tournament championship game, he scored 69 points. He had the complete package and by the time he turned eighteen, he was charming. He had this magnetic personality that everyone seemed to be enchanted by, and the girls were crazy about him. I would see him at the Rucker summer basketball tournament, lighting it up with jump shots and slam dunks. I think all of us who were younger wanted to be just like him.

Supreme had a friend called Tiny even though he was well over three hundred pounds, and a little taller than six feet. It was rumored in the hood that if you wanted to get high, he had what you needed. He had everything except marijuana. He said, "That shit don't do nothing but make you eat sweets all the time. The shit I got will make you feel like there's no worries and no pain, and you, brother Supreme you're bad, but this will make you badder."

"What's it called?" Supreme asked Tiny.

"Cocaine," replied Tiny, "but the street name is crack."

"Why do they call it crack?"

"Because it cracks open your brain and lets fresh air come through. I'ma give you some to try you'll see. There ain't no needles involved. All you need is a pipe with a bowl like this one"

"What's the bowl for?"

"That's how you cook it, but you don't inject nothing in your veins. You just take a nice breath of this and the world's a different place. You don't be noddin' like a junkie. Falling asleep standing up junkies look ridiculous. You just be mellow all day."

At first, Supreme was skeptical but when he realized there were no needles involved he gave it some thought.

"I tell you what, let's do some together then you'll know what I'm talking about," said Tiny. He had a little pipe with a bowl. He put some cocaine in the bowl, then took his lighter and cooked it until it was liquid. Supreme watched closely, it seemed harmless to him. Then when it was right, Tiny took a pull from the pipe then passed it to Supreme. Supreme took a pull. Just like Tiny said, he started feeling real mellow right away.

For a few years now, Harlem had become a playground for heavy drugs. People came from Jersey and other places to get their supply. Some folks called it medication from the street doctors to kill frustrations and worries disappointments and loneliness.

Now Supreme wasn't lonely even though his girl Cookie had just gone off to college. He had a lot of friends. He might have been a little frustrated because he didn't get an invite to an NBA camp after he had tried out.

He knew he was good enough. He was the purest shooter among the others at the try out.

Supreme's Harlem fans would chant his name when he came on the court, and he always did something that rocked the crowd. It seemed he could jump, and invent something while in mid-air. Right hand or left hand, he was good with both, and all the young and old hoopsters admired his game. *He was special.*

He wanted everyone to know he was ready to play pro ball maybe even play for the Knicks. *That was his dream.* He sat there in Tiny's SUV, and waited to be initiated into a world he had stayed away from but now he was curious. Tiny had a real swank SUV it was all hooked up. Once inside it was like you were sitting in someone's plush living room. Tiny kept it clean. Even in the winter with snow on the ground, his ride was clean inside out.

"Here man take another hit," Tiny exclaimed. When Supreme took the hit this time, he was even more amazed at the feeling—it seemed everything had slowed down and he could see everything so clearly. It was a hot day, but

Supreme felt a breeze. His frustrations were blowing in the breeze.

He knew he was good enough.

"I'll come off the street and go to try outs they'll have to pick me."

When Supreme got out of Tiny's SUV, he decided to walk down 125th Street, the most popular street in Harlem. All the tour buses in New York City always stopped there, and he too looked forward to the sights on 125th Street.

"Hi Joe." He recognized the voice. It was an old girlfriend, Monifa. She never called him Supreme even though she thought like everyone else that his game was truly that but she wanted to keep it personal.

"Hey what's up, I see you still looking good."

"You don't look too bad yourself" she responded. "Maybe we should get together sometime."

"Yeah, okay. You still have my number?"

"I know it by heart," he responded. "I'll give you a call."

Monifa was a cute girl, and since his real girl was away in school Supreme thought it might not be such a bad idea to rekindle an old flame. He hugged her and gave her a kiss on the cheek. "I'll call you."

"I'll be waiting," she said as she smiled and walked away.

Besides the fact that he was one of the best ballers in Harlem, Supreme could also draw. Sometimes he would draw cartoon characters of the teachers and the principal. A student gave the principal one of the drawings he had done just to see his reaction.

"This is very good even though he exaggerated my stomach a little bit. I like it," said the principal. To this day, he still has it on a wall in his office. He even encouraged Supreme to be in the district art contest, and told him, "Whatever you need, I'll get it for you." All Supreme needed was a big piece of canvas and some sponges, the school already had the paint.

Everyone wondered about the sponges. The sponges were the buildings in New York. He had the skyscrapers and the UN building and some smaller ones all done with sponges. It was brilliant.

Well, Supreme created a masterpiece and won first prize, and then gave it to the principal, which he put up in his office. Someone wanted to buy it, but the principal made it clear it was not for sale.

Supreme had talent. I think he could have done anything he wanted to, and do it well.

He was a good looking, talented kid with a charming personality. What more could you ask for? After his stroll down 125th Street, he decided to walk home.

Supreme lived on a quiet block lined with brownstones that were well taken care of that was referred to as Striver's Row. Everyone on the block looked out for each other. If you were a stranger standing around, someone would come and ask you who you were looking for. You didn't need police on Striver's Row, the people policed themselves. You could easily find Supreme's house because his mother had a green thumb. They had the prettiest bushes and flowers in the front yard. People would stop by just to admire the foliage.

When he got into his house, his father Joe Sr. said, "Joe, I want to talk to you."

"Okay Pops," he responded. He didn't like the way his father said it. Sounded like he had done something wrong.

His father came into the living room. "This is your senior year, right?"

"Right."

"What are your plans? What do you want to do ?"

"I want to play pro ball."

"You think you are ready for the pros?" his father asked.

"Yes I do. I've got a stronger game than some of the guys getting paid right now."

"But they're bigger and stronger than you son."

"But they can't shoot as well, and they can't jump as high as me." Supreme spoke with full confidence and conviction.

"You don't want to go to college and develop your body a little more?"

"I feel I'm ready now."

"So have you been invited to some pro tryouts?"

"No, but I know where the Garden is, and I know the Knicks have open tryouts."

"So you're gonna come off the street and go to the Knicks tryouts?"

"That's the plan."

"I've seen you play son, and you have a great game, but the pros are another story."

"I know pops, but I'm ready."

"I don't know how ready you are if you're gonna hang out with guys like Tiny."

Supreme was stunned. He didn't know his father knew he was hanging out with him. "You know what Tiny does and I don't think that helps your chances," his father continued.

"He's just a friend. I don't know what he does."

"The boy sells drugs. You're not messing with drugs, are you?"

"No pops."

His father looked at him with skeptical eyes. "Well if you're talking about turning pro, hanging out with Tiny is not going to help. I really wish you'd think about college."

"I want to make some real money, Pops. You don't get paid playing basketball in college."

"Okay son. I just hope you have a backup plan in case this doesn't work." He walked out of the room and left Supreme standing there thinking about what he had just said.

Supreme went upstairs to his room and laid down on his bed thinking. Just before he dozed off, his father came into his room and handed him a letter. "I think this is from Cookie" his father said.

Supreme couldn't wait to open it. His girl had written him and he was excited. She wrote about how much she liked it down there and her new friends. She said "all of us from New York hang together. I'm glad I got out of the city, they got trees down here. The only place we have trees is in the park in Harlem. I love Harlem but this is beautiful. I hope you come and visit me, I think you'll like it."

Supreme started imagining being with his girl down south. He sat on the side of his bed thinking about Cookie and looking at her picture. He fell asleep with her letter in his hand. Almost right away he started dreaming.

The dream was more like a nightmare. He was walking down 125th Street, and suddenly the cops rolled up on him, and did a body search. "He's clean," one officer said.

"How long have you known Robert Townsend. you know him as Tiny."

"He's a friend of mine."

"Well he's on his way to jail, and we thought you might know where his stash is since you were seen on two different occasions getting out of his SUV."

"I don't know anything about a stash."

"We're gonna have to check your house, and if we find anything, you're going to jail. Get in the car."

They drove to Supreme's house, spoke to his father then started searching the house. One police officer found a package with Supreme's name on it.

"What's this?" a cop asked

"I never saw that package before."

"Well lets see what's in it." They unwrapped the package and found at least a hundred viles of crack cocaine. "You say you don't know anything about this, huh?"

"I never saw this package before."

"It's got your name on it."

"But it's not mine." Supreme was damn near pleading.

"Well, it's got your name on it. Looks like we're going downtown, Mr. Ballplayer."

There were trophies around the house that showed his talents.

"Someone set me up."

"So this is a set up, huh?"

"Yeah, it's a set up. That's not my package."

They handcuffed him, and put him in the back seat of the squad car while his father stood there looking dejected and shaking his head.

"It's not mine I swear."

"We'll let the judge decide."

"I told you about hanging out with that boy," he coud hear his father as they drove off, with Supreme handcuffed in the backseat of the car. Then all of a sudden the phone rang, and woke Supreme up from this nightmare. It was Tiny of all people.

"Hey whatcha doin man?"

"I got some chores I gotta do"

"You know you're the only one I'd give free shit to. I got some more stuff for you if you can hang out."

"Not right now I've got some things I gotta do."

"Okay man, check you later." Tiny hung up.

Supreme felt relief when he realized it was all a dream. It was still very vivid in his mind. He decided right then he would never see Tiny again, and he thought seriously about taking that trip to see his girl Cookie. He also thought maybe going to college might be a good idea. It was time for a change of environment and a change of mind. ■

CHAPTER 14

My Shaw Narrative

AFTER I HAD FOUNDED and worked in the group, The Last Poets, I had no idea that Shaw University would play such an important role in my academic and social development.

It all started in 1969. I left The Last Poets a little over a year after we had started, and accepted a teaching job in North Carolina. I took my wife Biji and my son Pharoah, and went to a place that was used as a resort for some of the black ministers. It had been the home of one of the very first black junior colleges in America. The United Church of Christ decided to let the Committee for Racial Justice operate a school that would prepare black youngsters to attend a four-year college with academic skills that developed a black cultural awareness. I taught English and a creative writing class. There was African dance and drumming offered as well as African history classes. The school was located near Rocky Mount, in between the towns of Enfield and Whitaker.

We had a few introductory sessions with some of the prospective students and their parents. We even constructed some walls to make dorm space for those who would live on campus. Preparation lasted all summer, and we all looked forward to our first semester at our new school.

It never happened.

We were all given service money to return to New York, and a few of us were even given a job. I was one of the fortunate ones. I was given a job as a college developer and along with it came a house and a car, but I had to move to Raleigh, North Carolina and work at Shaw University. I couldn't wait to go to Shaw.

I had already been to a college in Iowa. I left after one year. My first college experience had been a real white one, so I was really looking forward to a real black experience. Shaw did not disappoint. In between my first year of college and Shaw, The Last Poets had been my express ticket to the Black Power movement. I had been known as Charles Davis most of my life (nicknamed Chuck), but now I embraced my African name, and refused to speak with my friends if they did not call me Abiodun.

When I arrived at Shaw in the fall semester of 1969, I just knew I was going to have a jolly black time. I quickly discovered that there was a lot of work to do. Many of the students were pledging Greek.

I was appalled.

All of my new African zeal became outraged over black people pledging something that had nothing to do with us. I would preach on the steps of the Student Union the need for us to have African Societies not Greek Fraternities and Sororities. So, I started the Yoruba Society at Shaw University. I had at least two dozen students join. The members adopted an African name and wore African garments. I would have weekly meetings on campus for recruiting purposes, and to let the other students know what we were all about. It was at one of those weekly meetings that I had two guys asking about guns in case we were attacked by the police,or the Klan for being so "African." I told them we were not about guns, but that getting a gun if necessary wasn't a problem.

The fact is I bought the bait and signed off on a plan to steal guns from the only two gun shops in Raleigh. The heist was for the most part successful, but two of my boys went back to retrieve weapons they had dropped. They didn't realize that they went back with an informant, and were quickly apprehended. I felt responsible because the caper was my idea. We had been stashing guns in Meserve Hall, but since I knew the police were getting a warrant to search, I got rid of all the guns. I was actually giving guns away. My major concern was getting my boys out of jail. I tried a number of things to get them released, but it all seem to rest with me.

I told Alex, one of the members, that I knew where we could get the money to get them out on bail and embarrass the KKK at the same time. I found out the place they held meetings, and when they collected dues. I was only hoping it would be enough money to get my boys out of jail. Alex and I had a new gun from the heist, so we decided to play gangsters. The robbery was successful until it came time to go—a Pepsi Cola van pulled up at the gas station. Both men got out and started heading toward the store, so we locked up the people in the store in the storage room. The two men soon discovered this, and came running out of the store. They went to their van and pulled out rifles and started shooting at us. We ran. Then I realized I had a gun too so I turned and fired. Then I heard no more sounds. I thought I must have killed someone. Alex and I got away from our plan to get back to the car, and were now in a heavily wooded area running for our lives.

Eventually we were caught and put in jail. We both got out on bail, and then came back to stand trial. The judge gave us 12-20 years in prison for armed robbery, our very first offense. After two years Alex and I got our custody changed from maximum to medium security, which allowed us to take advantage of the study release program. We both explained that we wanted to finish our college education.

In the fall of 1973, I started attending Shaw University as a full-time student. My reputation preceded me. I was treated with the utmost respect by the students and staff. and spent most of my time in the radio station. I created two programs, "Variations Phase 1" and "Variations Phase II." On both of my shows, I would start out reading fifteen-minute segments of *Native Son* by Richard Wright on the first hour, and *The Spook Who Sat By The Door* by Sam Greenlee at the beginning of my second hour. I read these books primarily because they were not allowed in prison.

Because I had created my own class schedule, I was on the campus very early in the morning and I didn't have to be back to the prison until 9:00 p.m. One day I got bored and put up a sign that said:

> IF YOU CAN SING, DANCE, ACT or WRITE POETRY
> meet me in the ballroom at 8:30 a.m.

Surprisingly, I had many more participants than I expected. I gave them poems to recite. Some of them recited their own. I had written a lot of poems and songs in prison, so I had them to offer as well. This was the birth of African Revolutionary Ensemble (ARE). We did a beautiful concert at the school and took our talents to neighboring colleges, as long as I could get back at the prison by 9:00 p.m. I could not afford to be late.

One of the groups highlights was opening up for the CHAVIS-DAVIS coming home celebration. Ben Chavis was released from jail on an appeal, and Angela Davis was out on parole. They both got together at Raleigh Memorial Auditorium for a big celebration and my group got a chance to open up for them.

Because of my Last Poets affiliation, I had access to a studio in mid-town Manhattan. We rented and borrowed cars to come to New York to record. The session produced a double album that everyone was proud of, but for some strange reason we never got it out.

I finally was released on parole, and I thought I would try to make North Carolina my home. ARE had a special gig coming up. We were to be the opening performers for a Stevie Wonder concert. We started imagining touring with Stevie. We knew once he heard us he was going to put us on. Stevie was scheduled to have a concert at the University of North Carolina in Chapel Hill; It never happened. Stevie got into a car accident in Salisbury, North Carolina and was in a coma for five days. We were devastated! All of our dreams seemed to die. I decided to go back to New York and ARE was no longer active.

Since I have the master tapes of the ARE recording, years later, I had cassette copies made, and gave each one to my children.

The Yoruba Society and ARE are two of the things that I'm most proud of while I was at Shaw. I have made many lasting friends, and I've got memories of some of the angels I met at Shaw, like O.A. Dupree. He was like a father to me and so many others. I have close friends who have left this planet, but their memories I will treasure forever. I will always be a SHAW BEAR. ■

CHAPTER 15

The Price of Luck

JUDY AND I HAD GONE TO COLOMBIA for my birthday. This was our third time going there. Colombia is a very laid back South American country with a reputation for exporting cocaine. When we first arrived in Bogotá, the cab driver told us about the assassination of six judges who were up against the drug cartel. "You can't have a trial without a judge," the cabbie said.

I remembered I started to take a picture of the courthouse, and armed guards appeared with their guns out with rifles aimed at me. They had a drug war going on, and they weren't taking any chances.

We walked around the city a bit then we went back to our hotel. I had noticed how Judy seemed a bit uncomfortable. When we were getting on the plane, she sat down rather funny. I asked her about it and she said she had swallowed a fish bone from some cheap fish she had bought and it seemed to be stuck in her system. She and I were hoping that it would eventually pass and she would be alright.

We rented a car and drove around getting a feel for the people and checking out the lovely architecture. Judy's trips were always a joy to me because she'd plan them thoroughly. Sometimes there was a trip inside a trip. This was one of those times. After a couple of days in Bogotá, we took a small plane to a beautiful island off the mainland named San Andres. San Andres was paradise. The water was a luscious blue, the sand was baby powder soft and the people were brown and friendly. I remember when we first arrived, I went to the liquor store to get some rum and ended up drinking and socializing with locals who didn't really care to wear shoes. Mostly everyone there spoke Spanish and English so communication was no problem.

It was obvious by their color that there was an African presence here. The slave trade went through South America before it arrived in North America, which was the last stop.

One of my biggest thrills when traveling is to meet nice people and have a good time like we've always been friends. When I got back to our hotel, Judy and I went right across the street from our hotel and had a rum and coke on the beach. We befriended a lady who owned a restaurant named Fernandez. She shared sweet treats with us for no cost. We decided that we would order a lobster dinner and have it on the terrace of our room, which was lovely. From the terrace you could see the people, the beach, and that massive body of water. It was a great view. After the lobster dinner was brought to our room, and placed on a table on the terrace, Judy got up and promptly fainted.

I was shocked. I did not think she was that ill. I tried reviving her. I got a cold cloth and put on her face and I kept talking to her. She wouldn't come to. I ran downstairs to the hotel lobby yelling "medico, medico." The lady at the check-in counter pointed to this guy who looked like a kid wearing sneakers and jeans. It was hard to believe he was a doctor. I got his attention and asked him to come with me to my room because my lady had fainted.

When we got to the room Judy was coming out of it but was still weak. He scoped out the room like a cop. "Were you using any drugs?" he asked. I told him the only thing we had was marijuana.

He quickly checked Judy then decided she needed to go to the hospital. We got her downstairs, and just before she got in the cab she almost fainted again.

I was worried.

Once we got to the hospital, I realized Dr. Mow was a well-respected doctor there. The nurses were running around like mice doing whatever he asked. He must have given her six bags of glucose to bring her back. Then he figured out what was wrong: Judy had food poisoning. He did an emergency operation to remove the fish bone. After a few hours he released her, and we went back to the hotel. Judy however was in no condition to play. She stayed in bed recuperating from a serious situation.

It just so happened that Dr. Mow and I became good friends. He would check on Judy from time to time, and we hung out. He took me to a gym where I got a chance to play basketball with some of the players from the national team—my jump shot was hot that day. I was even asked if I played professionally back in the states. I laughed and said no way. I saw a lot of the island and met some wonderful people.

That evening I decided to go to the only opened casino on the island. I'm usually pretty good at Blackjack, but tonight I couldn't lose. I do have a method, but this was over the top. At one point I had more chips in front of me than the dealer had in her tray. The head man came over to me and asked me if I smoked. I said, "No it's bad for your health." He explained I'm not talking about cigarettes, and

I said "Yes I smoke that." He suggested we go outside and smoke this big joint he had rolled up. I looked at my winnings. He said, "Don't worry about your money, you'll get every dime, just take a break for a minute."

We went on the beach and smoked this good herb. Then he said, "Look, I don't know what you're doing but right now you're busting the bank. We're the only casino on the island. There is another one but it's closed. Why don't you take a few days off and come back towards the end of the week."

This was brand new to me. I've had some nice winnings but I was never asked to stop playing before. I knew it was the work of the Gods. Just because Judy wasn't well, I had tremendous luck at the table, so I guess my birthday trip wasn't a complete bummer. I had never won that much money playing Blackjack. I decided I would do what Judy would do, and that was to go shopping.

Once we returned to Bogotá, I went shopping. I bought jeans and sweaters, and a gold necklace as well as a bracelet and some other small items. I was Santa for a day. I came back to the hotel loaded down with stuff. Most of what I bought was for Judy. After all, there would not have been a trip if she had not planned it. She had forced herself to come on the trip because she didn't want me to be disappointed. We left Bogotá with gifts from my winnings and Judy was making improvements. Dr. Mow had given her a prescription on a ripped off piece of paper, and I was able to get what she needed at the pharmacy without any problem.

I hadn't given Judy her jewelry. I wanted to make that the last thing I'd do before we departed. When the cab arrived in front of her building I opened up my suitcase and started looking for the jewelry. I was searching, but I couldn't find it. I ended up taking everything out of the bag because I knew it was there.

I couldn't believe it! I've been ripped off!

It could only have been someone who is handling the bags. Judy was happy with her other gifts, but the ones that I knew would bring her the biggest smile, maybe even a tear, was the jewelry. I couldn't believe it was gone. Judy asked me what was wrong and I told her, "Somebody went into my bag and stole your gifts."

She was sorry to hear that but then she said, "Buying jewelry is not your thing anyway." I was upset. A few days later I saw Black, a friend of my son's. He worked out at JFK airport. I asked him "Do workers out there go in people's bags and steal their valuables?"

Black said, "Yeah, if people are stupid enough to put valuables in their luggage." I was really upset now, because I knew I should have kept the stuff with me. Judy said she loved the sweaters and scarf I had given her, and that she was fine with that. I was still a little mad with myself. The jewelry was expensive. The fact is I still came home with a lot more money than I left with. I guess even if you're lucky, you have to pay a price.

Judy saw her personal doctor and he complimented Dr. Mow on the work he had done to help Judy get well. Her doctor told her she was fortunate to have a doctor at the hotel and he was a good one. Dr. Mow was an angel, right there when we needed him.

San Andres is a beautiful island with beautiful people. If given the time, I will revisit it someday. ■

CHAPTER 16

The Lady In My Life

I REMEMBER GROWING UP AS A CHILD in Queens, my mother (who was actually my aunt) had an award-winning flower garden. My father Daddy Joe and I were forbidden to do anything in her garden. It was off limits.

We had a nice piece of property and Daddy Joe sectioned off a part of it for a vegetable garden, and a place to work on trucks and cars. Mother's flower garden had gardenias, four o'clocks, roses, tulips, carnations, chrysanthemums, violets and tall elegant sunflowers in the back of the garden standing like sentinel guards overlooking everything. Mother really loved and cared for her garden. Everyone who saw it was impressed including Daddy Joe and me.

Mother was a Leo born August 12, and just like a lioness she protected her cubs. She nurtured and protected me just like she did her flowers. Her garden was simply a reflection of her nurturing nature and her appreciation for the finer things in life.

Before I met Judy, I had been married three times and quite a few relationships on the side. I guess you could say I was tending to the flowers in my garden. I started writing poetry because I thought it would be a clever way to attract young ladies. I think in many ways, I had an addiction to women. I knew this at an early age, and decided to attend an all boys high school (Haaren High School) so I could get my high school education without being distracted by the girls. I graduated with honors, but I still found time to flirt with women only in this case they were the teachers in my school.

I met Judy after I finished college (Shaw University). I was hired to teach children's literature at a newly developed college in New York City under the auspices of Antioch College in Yellow Springs Ohio. The school (The Teachers Incorporated), was designed to allow you to get a bachelors or a masters degree in early childhood education based on your work experience. Kwame, a good friend of mine, was the person who recommended me for the job. He introduced me to the administrative staff of which Judy was a part of.

It was clear when I first met her that she had struck a chord in me that I had never felt before. The feelings were mutual. She was a very attractive, tall caramel brown, elegantly dressed lady from the Sugar Hill section of Harlem. We started having lunch together almost everyday at Riverside Drive Park. We spent a lot of time talking, and just getting to know each other. I was really blown away when she told me her birthday which was the same day as Mother's, and felt right then and there that we were destined to be together.

Judy was also married with two sons, Peter and Paul. We knew we were violating our families and our vows by being together, but that didn't stop us. We were compelled to be together no matter what the circumstances were. We even called each other "Ace." This was the short version of that old Southern expression, "Ace Boon Coon." We really looked forward to each other's company.

During this time, my mother was in the hospital. She was a diabetic and was having a very difficult time. I wanted my mother to meet Judy. The first time I took her, Mother and Judy connected beautifully. I remember I had to meet with her doctor and left Judy alone with Mother. When I came back, Judy was braiding her hair.

While I never got a chance to meet Judy's mother in person, she knew about me, and I felt very close to her. Her sister Stephanie was a very good friend of mine who always offered good advice. Her father met me and knew there was something going on. I always felt he could look right through me.

During the thirty-nine years of our relationship, together we faced the loss of our family members. The two greatest losses were her younger sister, and her youngest son. Paul and I became very close especially after he started attending Syracuse University. Paul would arrange for me to perform at the school every year he was there, and I would always be handsomely paid.

Because of Judy, I have seen a lot of this world. I told her once when we were having a lunch date that I had a desire to celebrate my birthday some place where there was sun, sand and sea. The first trip we took was to Montego Bay, Jamaica. Every year after that, Judy would plan a surprise birthday trip on some island in the Caribbean or somewhere in South America. Most of the short stories in this book are about the places Judy and I have visited.

Judy could really read a map and loved to travel. Besides my annual birthday excursions, we traveled many places together. She would gauge how many miles I could drive in a day, and always have a place in mind where we could spend the night. I would drive and sing songs I had written. One of the best experiences we had traveling was the trip from Paris to Nice, then from Nice to Monte Carlo, and then from there to La Spezia, Italy. Judy had discovered this organization that provided vouchers that made it possible for us to have a hotel room and food for free. Many of the managers disliked the idea of honoring the voucher, but Judy had proof that their name was on the list. That was one of the most cost effective trips we've ever had. I remember it was the trip from Genoa to La Spezia where Judy turned me on to salad Nicosia, *the* perfect lunch on the road.

Speaking of food, this was just another one of Judy's talents. She had serious culinary art skills. She could cook and bake. Her lasagna and chili were special, and her carrot cake and brownies were something to die for. Judy was a blessing in so many ways. Despite her stunningly good looks, her infectious smile, her fabulous wardrobe, her warm personality and her pleasant voice, she did not like the limelight, she preferred being behind the scenes.

Judy spent most of her professional life working with children. Her love for children was something to admire. The love she shared with my children was more than appreciated by me and them.

She was such a thoughtful person. When she went shopping (she loved to shop), she didn't just shop for herself, but if she saw something she thought any of us would like she would just buy it. Judy had a motto that she lived by that she passed it on to me:"You've got to feel good about yourself." She lived by that and she showed it in everything she did.

Judy was the one person in my life who I loved more than any other, but my love for her didn't stop me from still admiring and tending to other flowers in the garden. I think I had some fear about being totally committed to just one person. One thing Judy always told me was that she never wanted to get in the way of me and my fans. I could be performing some place and talking to other women, but Judy never showed any jealousy.

As a matter of fact, I think one of the reasons our relationship endured was because she gave me my space. She lived uptown in Harlem with her son, and we never discussed the idea of living together. She knew I had to have my space, and that we should only be with each other when we wanted to. I stepped out of bounds a few times, but Judy understood my scandalous behavior, and always gave me some slack.

Many times I felt I did not deserve her. She was truly an angel, my angel.

She was spending the weekend with me when she passed away. She died in her sleep from complications with her heart. During our relationship, I was with her when her parents died, her sister and her son Paul died. It was very difficult for me to accept that she had moved on as well. I have come to realize in these last couple of years the spirit is more powerful than the flesh. I miss her touch and all the things she did for me, but I still communicate with her, and she still helps me live my life.

Judy was a very positive person about life and death, and her love is teaching me even now how to be the same. She is my special sunflower standing in the back of the garden watching over everything I do. ■

CHAPTER 17

Judy

How do you describe an angel
What human body
Can house the spirit of a saint
Judy was all that to me and more
She gave me fresh air to breathe
And a view of the world
I had not seen before.

With her smile as bright as the sun
This tall lean caramel brown diva
Didn't sing or dance
Her presence was art itself.

Her wisdom helped me grow
Her love let me know
I was blessed by her touch
Healed by the sound of her voice
She found ways to take me to heaven
And showed me how to fly.

Even in an unhappy moment
She always found the good
Didn't hang out with ugly
Beauty was her friend.

Angels don't stay here forever
We hate to see them go
But they've got to go
So they can come back.

Judy's gone now
Food don't taste the same
The brownies are not as sweet
All the bright colors look faded now
Because Judy had to return to heaven.

I am happy to have had
This angel in my life
She reminds me everyday
That God is on my side
And her love will always be my shelter.

CHAPTER 18

The Legacy of The Last Poets

THE LAST POETS EMERGED during the Black Power movement, a movement that emphasized racial pride, and the creation of black political and cultural institutions to nurture and promote black collective interests. In the process, a black arts aesthetic developed to advance black values through literature, poetry, dance, music, theatre and the visual arts. We sought to create politically engaging work that explored the black cultural and historical experience, by transforming how black people see themselves in a more positive light.

The Last Poets was modeled after the West African griot tradition. We delivered stories rhythmically, over drums and sparse instrumentation, which for many is considered the precursor of rap and hip hop. There were other artists out there doing similar work, like Gil Scott Heron and The Watts Prophets, who were dedicated to educating and entertaining the black masses.

When *The Last Poets,* our first album hit the streets, it did exceedingly well, and while I was still in prison, Umar and Jalal Mansur Nuriddin were enjoying its success. In the meantime, Gylan Kain, David Nelson and Felipe Luciano were not happy. They had once been in the group, but they were not getting the play that the other members were receiving. So there were physical fights in the street over who the real Last Poets were. My wife would keep me informed, but there was nothing I could do to stop this madness.

In an effort to usurp what Umar and Jalal were doing, Gylan, David and Felipe did their own album entitled, *Right On the Original Last Poets,* however nothing could stop the surge of the first album. It sold a million copies by word of mouth. Eventually, Umar and Jalal connected with another brother named Sulaiman El Hadi to keep the trinity alive. They recorded two albums, and had some degree of success.

It was in the early 1990s when hip hop became more prominent that a lawyer out of Detroit, Gregory J. Reed, got in touch with David, Kain, Felipe and myself to get back together. He wanted to bring us to Detroit to receive a proclamation, appear in some of the schools, and have a black tie concert at Orchestra Hall. The effort to bring us back fell short. Kain had moved to Amsterdam and was not moving back to America. There were arguments about money that we had not even received yet. We even did a recording that never got released. We did one other gig together at Kent State in Ohio in commemoration of the students who were killed by the National Guard some twenty years before.

After this failed effort, I turned to my music. I had been writing a lot of songs and performing with a group I started at Shaw University called ARE (African Revolutionary Ensemble). We would perform all over North Carolina at various schools. We even recorded a double album that was never released. When I moved back to New York, I started a jazz group called Griot. We performed at colleges, community centers and various clubs. I was also teaching at Columbia University. I was raising a family. Years had gone by, and I wasn't even thinking about The Last Poets. Then in 1995, Umar Bin Hassan paid me a surprise visit one afternoon.

I always say that in the absence of a movement, the circus comes to town.

Back then, during the 1960s and 1970s, the focus was about uplifting people and building black unity. Today, the focus is on money. The Black Power movement petered out in the mid-1970s due to lack of continuity of leadership and participants, against the backdrop of the powerful, changing times, and with it the popularity of The Last Poets had declined. All of this coincided with the downfall of the black consciousness movement in America: the FBI's Cointelpro program had infiltrated all the major black political organizations, the Black Panther party was in disarray, and drugs were flooding our neighborhoods. Artists who achieved cultural recognition and economic success as their works began to be celebrated by the white mainstream, were no longer part of the collective.

With no movement to bring black people together, black folks worked individually to bring themselves up by the bootstraps, which has had mixed results. By the decadent 1980s, it was every man for himself, which is probably the reason why The Last Poets did very little during this time period. Interestingly, it was during this decade that The Last Poets became renown with the rise of hip hop music, often being name-checked as grandfathers and founders of the new movement.

I hadn't seen Umar in twenty years. Here he was talking about "taking our crown back." I had heard Umar had a bout with drugs, but it had not diminished his skills—his poetry was better than ever. I had always given him credit for writing a classic on the first album, "Niggers Are Scared of Revolution," but he had some other poems that were equally potent. I decided to give it a go and see where this effort would take us.

You see, the message from the young rappers today is different from The Last Poets.

In the meantime, hip hop devolved into a different kind of craft. Reciting poetry with music, rap and spoken word began as a producer based art form among working class and poor black youth. When hip hop transformed into a global consumer product in the 1990s, record executives began to urge hip hop artists to write more violent and offensive lyrics at the demand of hip hop audiences. Misogynistic and gangsta-laden lyrics made its way into an art form that was initially developed as a means to communicate social and political ideas to the masses, at the expense of black people and our culture.

These days, there are few culturally-conscious hip hoppers and rappers who have directly addressed the social, cultural, and political issues that affect people in everyday life. Umar and I have recorded with a few of these conscious rappers like Common, Chuck D, Nas and Melle Mel.

I'd like to think that hip hop will improve, but I think the misogyny and violence is part of a bigger problem in the black community. *And then there is the money.*

Hip hop evolved into a money machine that drives several markets, most notably the advertising industry. In order for change to happen, the fans will have to want it, and more importantly, the artists will have to want to create tangible art that is meaningful. It is my hope that just as The Last Poets have been credited as the forbearer of hip hop, that our legacy will remind spoken word artists, rappers and hip hop artists that all of this began as a West African griot tradition of telling stories, fables and truths.

Black people have been through a lot. It seems instead of moving forward, we've only made incremental gains. We seem to be stuck.

With the collapse of the Black Power movement, I have often pondered for years about what black people must do to move forward. When Black Lives Matter boldly organized as a hashtag on Twitter several years ago, I saw some hope. When they elected to not be led by a single leader or develop a centralized leadership structure, I immediately recognized some of the same mistakes we made back in the day. The fact that they were able to raise black consciousness from the streets to the White House (under Obama) is impressive, so I remain hopeful. Because, as an old Nationalist, I still believe that a movement is very much needed to help nurture and promote black collective interests. The same things we fought for during the 1960s—police brutality, poverty and social injustice—ring true even now. The difference is that today our concerns have grown into an international awareness that has crossed racial lines, but in order to succeed we need to get organized and stay on course for the long haul.

Twenty-eight years have passed since Umar first knocked on my door, and we have been all over the world since. Umar and I happen to be the youngest members of The Last Poets fraternity, and we are also both from Ohio. We don't always get along, but we know how to get it done on the stage. Our conga player is a brother named Donald "Babatunde" Eaton; he is also a priest in the Yoruba religion like our old conga player, Nilaja Obabi, who passed away some years ago. Babatunde is our heart beat.

Since this latest incarnation of The Last Poets, Umar and I have recorded a number of albums. We also published a book entitled, *On A Mission: Selected Poems and a History of The Last Poets* (1996), which provides the back story of many of the classic poems we have written. Bill Laswell has produced our most recent work. With him we have had done some outstanding recording sessions with some of the heavy weights in the industry like George Clinton, Bootsy Collins and the late Bernie Worwell.

Umar and I also participated on a Grammy nominated track, "The Corner" (2005), with Common. We also did a documentary with filmmaker Claude Santiago in Paris, *The Last Poets /made in Amerikkka* (2011), with all The Last Poets except Gylan Kain. We also had the wonderful opportunity to perform at Radio City Music Hall with Erykah Badu, and Christine Otten, a Dutch writer, wrote a book called, *The Last Poets* (2016).

Whenever and wherever we perform, I never fail to mention all of the poets who have graced the stage as The Last Poets. I believe it is important and respectful to give credit to those who made significant contributions in making this group legendary. I refer to David Nelson, who is now Dahveed, as the father of the group because it was his idea. I give credit to Gylan Kain for giving us our aesthetic. You had to write real poetry to be a Last Poet, and Gylan was a serious taskmaster, and he knew the craft.

Felipe bridged the gap between blacks and our Latino brothers and sisters who acknowledged the African blood flowing through their veins. I give credit to Sulaiman El Hadi for his storytelling style of poetry that always made you think. I have always believed that Jalal had the biggest impact on hip hop because everybody rhymes and that's all he did.

I refer to Umar's poem, "Niggers Are Scared of Revolution" as the anthem for the group. More importantly, his style of delivery is very unique and probably the most copied. When it comes to my contribution, I would say I'm very versatile because I can sing, and I usually do at all of our concerts.

The Last Poets are a group of men from different walks of life who decided to come together to impact a serious change in the lives of black people everywhere. Initially, our mission was to "kill the niggers" in us and emerge as black people who have respect and love for one another. Our mission today has elevated to recognize that the whole world needs raising. Humanity in general is taking a beating. The machine is taking over. We're not sensitive enough to our needs or each other. Umar puts it best when he says, "We all just want to be loved, appreciated and respected." Even now it seems like an impossible task to achieve.

Being a Last Poet for fifty years has provided me with gifts I could never imagine. I was very surprised to learn that the average hip hop kid knows who we are. The love and respect I receive every time I visit a classroom or another country is overwhelming. I am more than grateful for the opportunities it has afforded me.

The Last Poets also taught me how to be artistically free and not be beholden to anyone. I am very lucky that the work Umar and I have produced over the years has remained relevant. It has afforded me the opportunity to teach and lecture on my terms. Ultimately, the story of The Last Poets is about human resilience, and the beauty of being true to oneself.

The beauty of being. ■

ABOUT THE POET

PHOTO CREDIT: Vagabond

ABIODUN OYEWOLE is a poet, teacher, and founding member of the American music and spoken-word group, The Last Poets (1968), which laid the groundwork for the emergence of hip hop. He performed on The Last Poets' albums, *The Last Poets* (1970), *Holy Terror* (1993), and *The Time Has Come* (1997). Oyewole rejoined The Last Poets during its 1990s resurgence, and co-authored with Umar Bin Hassan, *On A Mission: Selected Poems and a History of The Last Poets* (1996). He released the rap CD, *25 Years* (1996), published his first poetry collection with 2Leaf

Press, *Branches of The Tree of Life: The Collected Poems of Abiodun Oyewole 1969-2013* (2014), and is the editor of *Black Lives Have Always Mattered, A Collection of Essays, Poems, and Personal Narratives* (2017). He released the song albums, *Gratitude* (Sons Rising Entertainment, 2014), and *Love Has No Season* (2014). Oyewole received his BS in biology and BA in communications at Shaw University, an MA in education at Columbia University, and is a Columbia Charles H. Revson Fellow (1989). Over the years, Oyewole has collaborated on more than a dozen albums and several books. He writes poetry almost every day, travels around the world performing poetry, teaches workshops, gives lectures on poetry, history and politics; and holds a weekly salon for artists, poets and writers in his home in Harlem, New York.■

OTHER BOOKS BY 2LEAF PRESS

2LEAF PRESS challenges the status quo by publishing alternative fiction, non-fiction, poetry and bilingual works by activists, academics, poets and authors dedicated to diversity and social justice with scholarship that is accessible to the general public. 2LEAF PRESS produces high quality and beautifully produced hardcover, paperback and ebook formats through our series: *2LP Explorations in Diversity, 2LP University Books, 2LP Classics, 2LP Translations, Nuyorican World Series,* and *2LP Current Affairs, Culture & Politics.* Below is a selection of 2LEAF PRESS' published titles.

2LP EXPLORATIONS IN DIVERSITY

Substance of Fire: Gender and Race in the College Classroom
by Claire Millikin
Foreword by R. Joseph Rodríguez, Afterword by Richard Delgado
Contributed material by Riley Blanks, Blake Calhoun, Rox Trujillo

Black Lives Have Always Mattered
A Collection of Essays, Poems, and Personal Narratives
Edited by Abiodun Oyewole

The Beiging of America:
Personal Narratives about Being Mixed Race in the 21st Century
Edited by Cathy J. Schlund-Vials, Sean Frederick Forbes, Tara Betts
with an Afterword by Heidi Durrow

What Does it Mean to be White in America?
Breaking the White Code of Silence, A Collection of Personal Narratives
Edited by Gabrielle David and Sean Frederick Forbes
Introduction by Debby Irving and Afterword by Tara Betts

2LP UNIVERSITY BOOKS
Designs of Blackness, Mappings in the Literature and
Culture of African Americans
A. Robert Lee
20TH ANNIVERSARY EXPANDED EDITION

2LP CLASSICS
Adventures in Black and White
Edited and with a critical introduction by Tara Betts
by Philippa Duke Schuyler

Monsters: Mary Shelley's Frankenstein and Mathilda
by Mary Shelley, edited by Claire Millikin Raymond

2LP TRANSLATIONS
Birds on the Kiswar Tree
by Odi Gonzales, Translated by Lynn Levin
Bilingual: English/Spanish

Incessant Beauty, A Bilingual Anthology
by Ana Rossetti, Edited and Translated by Carmela Ferradáns
Bilingual: English/Spanish

NUYORICAN WORLD SERIES
Our Nuyorican Thing, The Birth of a Self-Made Identity
by Samuel Carrion Diaz, with an Introduction by Urayoán Noel
Bilingual: English/Spanish

Hey Yo! Yo Soy!, 40 Years of Nuyorican Street Poetry,
The Collected Works of Jesús Papoleto Meléndez
Bilingual: English/Spanish

LITERARY NONFICTION
No Vacancy; Homeless Women in Paradise
by Michael Reid

The Beauty of Being, A Collection of Fables, Short Stories & Essays
by Abiodun Oyewole
WHEREABOUTS: Stepping Out of Place,
An Outside in Literary & Travel Magazine Anthology
Edited by Brandi Dawn Henderson

PLAYS
Rivers of Women, The Play
by Shirley Bradley LeFlore, with photographs by Michael J. Bracey

AUTOBIOGRAPHIES/MEMOIRS/BIOGRAPHIES
Trailblazers, Black Women Who Helped Make America Great
American Firsts/American Icons
by Gabrielle David

Mother of Orphans
The True and Curious Story of Irish Alice, A Colored Man's Widow
by Dedria Humphries Barker

Strength of Soul
by Naomi Raquel Enright

Dream of the Water Children:
Memory and Mourning in the Black Pacific
by Fredrick D. Kakinami Cloyd
Foreword by Velina Hasu Houston, Introduction by Gerald Horne
Edited by Karen Chau

The Fourth Moment: Journeys from the Known to the Unknown, A Memoir
by Carole J. Garrison, Introduction by Sarah Willis

POETRY
PAPOLíTICO, Poems of a Political Persuasion
by Jesús Papoleto Meléndez
with an Introduction by Joel Kovel and DeeDee Halleck

Critics of Mystery Marvel, Collected Poems
by Youssef Alaoui, with an Introduction by Laila Halaby

shrimp
by jason vasser-elong, with an Introduction by Michael Castro
The Revlon Slough, New and Selected Poems
by Ray DiZazzo, with an Introduction by Claire Millikin

Written Eye: Visuals/Verse
by A. Robert Lee

A Country Without Borders: Poems and Stories of Kashmir
by Lalita Pandit Hogan, with an Introduction by Frederick Luis Aldama

Branches of the Tree of Life
The Collected Poems of Abiodun Oyewole 1969-2013
by Abiodun Oyewole, edited by Gabrielle David
with an Introduction by Betty J. Dopson

2Leaf Press is an imprint owned and operated by the Intercultural Alliance of Artists & Scholars, Inc. (IAAS), a NY-based nonprofit organization that publishes and promotes multicultural literature.

NEW YORK
www.2leafpress.org